ANNIE M.P. SMITHSON (1873-1948) was the most successful of all Irish romantic novelists. Her nineteen books, including Nora Connor, Paid in Full, The Walk of a Queen, Her Irish Heritage, *and* The Marriage of Nurse Harding *were all bestsellers, with their wholesome mix of old-fashioned romance, spirited characters and commonsense philosophy.*

She was born in Sandymount, Co. Dublin, and reared in the strict Unionist tradition. On completion of her training as a nurse in London and Edinburgh, she returned to Dublin and was posted north as a Queen's Nurse in 1901. Here, for the first time, she experienced the divide between Irish Nationalists and Unionists, and it appalled her. She converted to Catholicism at the age of 34 and was subsequently disowned by most of her family. She immersed herself in the Republican movement — actively canvassing for Sinn Féin in the 1918 General Election, nursing Dubliners during the influenza epidemic of that year, instructing Cumann na mBan on nursing care and tending the wounded of the Civil War in 1922. She was arrested and imprisoned, and threatened to go on hunger-strike unless released.

Forced to resign her commission in the strongly Loyalist Queen's Nurses Committee, she took up private work and tended the poor of Dublin city until she retired in 1942. During her long career, she did much to improve the lot of the nursing profession and championed its cause as Secretary of the Irish Nurses Union.

In later years, she devoted herself to her writing and was an active member of WAAMA, PEN and the Old Dublin Socity, Her autobiography, Myself — and Others, *was completed in 1944, four years before her death at the age of 75.*

PAID IN FULL

By

Annie M.P. Smithson

THE MERCIER PRESS

The Mercier Press, Cork

First Published by The Talbot Press
This edition (c) The Mercier Press 1990

ISBN 978 1 78117 929 1

The characters in this story are purely fictitious. No reference is intended, by name or implication, to any person, living or dead.

Typeset by Seton Music Graphics Ltd., Bantry, Co. Cork
Transferred to Digital Print-on-Demand in 2024

CONTENTS

I	*First Meeting*	7
II	*Summer Idyll*	13
III	*Mary Gilfoyle*	19
IV	*The Shadow from the Past*	25
V	*Lilac Tree House*	31
VI	*Margaret Conroy*	38
VII	*A Bolt from the Blue*	45
VIII	*Nora Makes Up Her Mind*	52
IX	*Rose Hears some News*	58
X	*'What Is Your Name?'*	63
XI	*Teresa Mason*	71
XII	*Harold is Puzzled*	79
XIII	*Nemesis*	85
XIV	*Christmas Eve*	89
XV	*An Invitation*	96
XVI	*An Old Fenian Goes Home*	103
XVII	*A New Venture*	108
XVIII	*The Wheel of Fortune Turns*	119
XIX	*The Message*	127
XX	*Renunciation*	133

| XXI | *Teresa Takes a Hand* | 139 |
| XXII | *A Christmas Gift for Nora* | 146 |

CHAPTER 1

FIRST MEETING

Rain—rain—nothing but rain, falling steadily from a leaden sky. The Esplanade was deserted, the whole sea front looked desolate and deserted.

Nora Tiernan, gazing at such a picture from the window of her seaside lodging, was feeling distinctly aggrieved. She had come to Bray for her fortnight's holiday and already three precious days had gone by—and every one of them had been wet. She had a room in a small cottage at the foot of Bray Head which had been recommended to her by one of the girls in the office. It was a pleasant little bed-sittingroom, and the landlady seemed a good sort. But all the same, she had not come to Bray to sit at the window looking out at rain falling into the grey sea. That same sea had been blue as the skies above it on the first evening of her arrival—but had never been blue since. For two days she had been indoors and she was sick of it. In desperation she put on her raincoat and pixie and sallied forth. She would see how far she could go up the Head. It was not windy, just raining—raining. Many a girl would have thought nothing of climbing the Head in such weather—would even have enjoyed the walk. But Nora Tiernan was not what is known as an outdoor girl. She had been rather delicate as a child, and although she had outgrown all that long ago, her parents, while they were alive, had rather spoilt and indulged her. She was their only child, and so anxious were they about her, that she was not even allowed to play games or go for hikes as she sometimes wished to do. And then when Nora was only eighteen, they had both died within a short time of each other, and the girl was left practically alone in the world. That had been a terrible time and Nora did not like to think about it even now after three years.

Her father had been a solicitor in a good practice, but—with the help of an extravagant wife—he had lived up to every penny of his income, and beyond it. Then he had endeavoured to retrieve his fortunes by gambling on the Stock Exchange, with the result that he had lost not only his own money but also that belonging to a client which he had been tempted to use. It had been a very considerable sum too, and the client in consequence became a poor man. The disappointment and the fear of discovery—which he knew must inevitably come—unhinged John Tiernan's mind, and in a moment of desperation he shot himself. His wife—who with all her faults had been devoted to him—only survived him for a few weeks. And so their beloved daughter was left alone in the world with—as far as she knew—no near living relative. Mrs. Tiernan had been an only child, her parents were dead, and her only relations some distant cousins in England. Mr. Tiernan's two brothers were dead, and his sister had gone to Australia when a girl and he had heard nothing of her for many years. The furniture of the pretty Rathgar house was sold, as was everything else which had once belonged to John Tiernan. The proceeds were divided amongst his creditors. The one who suffered most and who had lost heavily was the client whose money he had been tempted to use. The fact that he never meant to be dishonest made no difference to the law in whose eyes he was a thief, one who had taken money belonging to another, and worse still, money which had been entrusted to him.

So Nora was left penniless. Yet not quite. On that terrible morning when John Tiernan had been found lying dead in his study, his daughter—before she knew of the tragedy—had been surprised to find a letter addressed to herself in his handwriting. She opened it wonderingly and found a bank note for fifty pounds, with the following words written on a half sheet of paper: 'My dear child. When you get this you will know that I have taken the coward's way out. I could not face what was coming to me. Take this money, it is all I can leave you. It is hard for you—reared as you have been—but you will have only yourself now. My heart is breaking when I think of what my folly has brought upon you. Go to Cecil Derwent and take his advice in everything. I can write no more.'

Afterwards Nora sometimes thought it strange that her father had made no mention of her mother, he had written as if she were already alone in the world—as alone she was to be in such a short time. Was it that some premonition had told him that his wife was shortly to follow him? The letter had been left on Nora's dressing-table, which meant that he must have come to her room while she was asleep. Poor man! What desolation and bitterness must have been his as he gazed for the last time at his beloved child.

Just at first, Nora had been too dazed, too overwhelmed by the tragedy to understand what it all meant. That her father—that

First Meeting

dear daddy whom she so idolised—should have done this thing seemed unbelievable to her. Her only consolation was that he had not known what he was doing at the time.

At the inquest the verdict had been 'suicide while temporarily insane.' It was the only comfort left to his daughter.

All this had happened three years ago when Nora had been barely eighteen. She had gone to her father's friend, Cecil Derwent, for advice, and he had indeed proved to be a friend in need to the girl. When her mother died—a brokenhearted woman if ever there was one—he and his wife had insisted that Nora should stay with them in their pretty house at Rathfarnham. She stayed with them for nearly a year, and with her fifty pounds she paid for a course at one of the commercial colleges. She became a good shorthand-typist, and although Cecil Derwent was an artist and had little interest in business, yet he knew a good many business people in the city. So when Nora had finished her training and was ready for work, he spoke to several of these men. It was then that he got his first set-back—and Nora too. She was her father's daughter, the daughter of a suicide and a dishonest man—one who had used money which did not belong to him—gambling his client's money on the Stock Exchange. They did not care to employ his daughter in their office. When several firms had replied in this way, Cecil Derwent advised Nora to change her surname. He felt that it was the only thing to do. He knew that she was a good worker and would be conscientious in every way. But the stigma attached to her father's name remained with her. Even although he had been pronounced insane, hard businessmen argued that he had not been so when he had made use of money which was not his own.

For a while Nora had refused to do as her friend suggested. But as the days went by and she could get no work she gave way. Her father's full name had been John Malcolm Tiernan—Malcolm had been the family name of his mother's father, and he had been called by it to please the old man. But Mr. Tiernan had seldom used it and was always known as John Tiernan. Now his daughter was known as 'Miss Malcolm', and nobody associated her with the John Tiernan of three years ago. She had answered an advertisement for a typist in the office of a big seed merchant and had got the post. She had now been working there for nearly two years. Her friends, the Derwents, had gone to Belgium for a holiday in this year of 1936, before the havoc of war had devastated Europe, and Nora missed them sadly. They had asked her to go with them, but somehow she wished for an independent holiday all alone. She had a bed-sittingroom in Rathmines and looked after herself, preferring this to staying in a boarding house, like most of the other girls. Nora was not one to make friends easily, and since her father's death had kept very much to herself. Courteous and kind always to the other girls working with her, she had made no real friends. The fact that she had been compelled to take another name, made her feel as if she were living under a cloud—and would do so all her life. It had made the girl older than her years and had deprived her of that light-heartedness and gaiety of spirit which is the right of all young people.

She was thinking over these things as she took the path along Bray Head. She did not often let her mind dwell upon the past, she knew it was not healthy to do so, and she was, as a rule, so busy—her work occupied her so fully—that she had little time to allow herself to dwell upon that terrible period in her life. At the end of the day she was tired, and when she had cooked her evening meal and tidied up, was only too glad to relax with a book.

Young men did not attract her in the least, and when she heard the others in the office talking about their 'boy friends', she was bored and uninterested. She treated herself sometimes to the theatre when there was a good play or the opera, but seldom went to the pictures.

This was the first holiday she had taken alone. Last summer she had stayed for her fortnight's leave with the Derwents, but now she was alone and had taken these lodgings in Bray on the advice of one of the girls in the office. She had found them comfortable enough, indeed if the weather had been good so that she could have been out of doors most of the time, she would have enjoyed the rest and change. But this wretched rain, so dismal at the seaside and looking as though it would never cease—this had damped her spirits as much as it was damping everything else. So her thoughts were inclined to be sombre and grey as she trudged along in the wet.

Sad enough meditations for the first days of her holidays. But it was the weather—so she told herself. Who could be cheerful or bright in this rain? She walked a good bit up the Head and then turned to come back, for the rain was, if anything, heavier than ever.

First Meeting

It was very lonely. There had seemed to be no one but herself on the Head, so that presently she was surprised to hear quick footsteps coming behind her. A moment later a young man drew abreast with her.

'I beg your pardon,' he said, raising his cap, 'but I wonder if you could tell me the right time? My watch is stopped.'

Nora glanced at her wristlet watch—a present from her father in those far-off happy days.

'It is just a quarter past twelve,' she said.

'Thanks so much. It's awkward not to know the time—isn't it?'

Nora assented rather shyly. But if she were shy, this young man was certainly not afflicted with the same failing. He fell into step beside her and started to make conversation in an easy manner.

'Beastly weather—isn't it?' he said. Adding: 'I suppose, like myself, you are here for a holiday?'

'Yes,' replied Nora, 'I only came three days ago—and it has rained ever since!'

'What rotten luck! And have you much longer to stay?'

'Only ten days—that's all.'

'Well let us hope the weather will improve, for after all a holiday at the sea depends on the weather—doesn't it?'

'It certainly does,' replied Nora, 'but surely this wet weather cannot last much longer?'

'It is hard to say, but we must only hope for the best. I am a bit better off than you, as I have a month's leave, and this is only the first week.'

'How lucky for you!'

They continued down the Head, side by side, he evidently taking it for granted that they should do so. Nora stole a glance at him now and then. He was tall, well-set-up young fellow, with wavy fair hair that many a girl might have envied, and blue eyes with a perpetual twinkle in their depths. On his part he gazed quite frankly at the girl beside him, admiring her dark eyes and what he could see of her face beneath her pixie. As they reached Naylor's Cove—so crowded with bathers and pleasure seekers on a fine day but now practically deserted—he asked her if she were staying on the Front? Rather surprised, she replied a trifle coldly in the affirmative. However, he did not ask for further details, but as he kept by her side until she reached Mrs. Brennan's cottage, there was no need for him to do so.

'Well, we shall doubtless meet again,' he said, smiling. 'My name, by the way, is Harold Hastings.'

He looked at her as if waiting for a similar introduction on her part. She could not help liking him, and replied quietly: 'I am Nora Malcolm.'

As she spoke, the girl coloured rather painfully, and he wondered why she did so. The reason—which of course he could not know—was that when she gave that name she always felt ashamed—almost guilty—even now, after two years.

'Well, good morning, Miss Malcolm,' said Harold Hastings, lifting his cap, 'here's to our next meeting—and let us hope that it will be in the sun—and not in the rain!'

Then he was gone, and Nora went in to change her wet things and listen to Mrs. Brennan's protests against going out in such weather.

CHAPTER II
SUMMER IDYLL

The next morning the rain had gone, and Nora saw a very different picture from the previous day as she looked out of her window. Overhead was a cloudless blue sky which was reflected in the blue waters beneath. Already people were out on the Esplanade and early bathers could be seen on their way to the sea. Nora dressed quickly, and was just putting the finishing touches to her toilet when Mrs. Brennan entered with her breakfast.

'Good morning, Miss. That's a better day, thank God,' she said.

'Yes, indeed,' agreed Nora, 'I'm so glad the rain has gone.'

Her breakfast finished, Nora took her bathing things and made her way up the Head to Naylor's Cove. She liked bathing there, it was such a lovely spot—she only hoped it would not be too crowded, as it often was when she had come down to Bray on her Saturday afternoons after the office. But now—early in the week and at this comparatively early hour—the beach was quiet enough. Later on, no doubt, it would be quite noisy.

Nora had her swim and then sat down on the sands with her book. It was delightful there in the sun—such a change to yesterday—she would enjoy her rest and a good story.

But somehow the book did not hold her interest. She found her thoughts wandering back to yesterday—to the young man she had met on the Head in the pouring rain, and who had introduced himself as Harold Hastings. Rather an attractive name, she thought, and he was decidedly attractive himself. It was queer that she should be thinking so much about him, for she seldom took any interest in the opposite sex—it had been a standing joke in the office. And yet she had thought of this man last thing when going to bed last night, she had dreamt about him—and now here she was letting her thoughts dwell upon him again—wondering if they would meet again as he had said. Perhaps they might. Summer visitors to Bray generally frequented the same places and often met— even several times in the one day. So why should they not meet?

And it was while she was thus thinking that she heard his voice behind her.

'Good morning, Miss Malcolm,' he said, as he flung himself on the sands beside her. 'So we have met again—and in the sun, too! This is better than yesterday—isn't it?'

'It is, indeed,' she agreed, with an answering smile.

'Yes—rather a different outlook this morning,' he went on. 'Have you bathed? But I see you have,' with a glance at her wet bathing togs spread to dry.

'Yes, I like to be early when the tide suits. What about you?'

'Oh, I had a swim before breakfast. The tide was just coming in—it was grand.'

They sat there, talking away as if they had been old friends, now and then exchanging jokes about some of the bathers. Nora, usually so reserved with strangers, found herself talking away to this man as if she had known him for years. He told her that he was in a solicitor's office, had passed his examinations, and had hopes of a partnership later on.

'The worst of it is, I have no money,' he said with a sigh, 'but Mr. Grey was a great friend of my father's, and as he is an old bachelor, he may overlook that fact and take me on as a partner—in fact he has as good as hinted as much.'

He also told Nora that his father was dead but his mother was still alive, living with her sister in the country.

'I wanted her to join me here for a month,' he said, 'but she will not leave Aunt Annabella who is very delicate. I go down to them—they live near the town of Wexford—at Christmas and Easter, and so on.'

In return Nora told him where she was working and how much she had looked forward to this little holiday.

'A fortnight is very short,' he said, 'they should give you a month.'

'Oh, but I am only a junior as yet,' she said.

'The senior girls get a month, and I expect I shall get it too when I have been there for some years.'

'If you stay so long,' he said.

For an instant her heart stood still. What did he mean by that? He did—he could not—know her secret. Know that she always went in deadly fear that someone would recognise her as John Tiernan's daughter and tell her employers, and then Mr. Cannon, the business manager, would ask her to step into Mr. Murphy's office and the head of the firm would tell her that she must go—that they could not keep her in the office any longer—she who was the daughter of a suicide and a thief. Always, always, was that terror before her. It had been a nightmare for over two years now.

Harold Hastings, glancing at her when she did not reply, noticed how pale she had become.

'Miss Malcolm!' he asked, 'are you not well? Is the sun too hot? Perhaps you would like a shadier place?'

That it had been his remark that had upset her never for an instant crossed his mind. By his words he had simply meant that she would probably be married before many years had passed—a pretty girl like her and with such nice ways, too. He looked at some of the girls lying on the sands,'sun bathing,' in very scanty bathing togs. He was no prude, but he did not like to see girls making themselves so cheap, stepping down from that pedestal upon which every decent-minded man has placed Womanhood.

But Nora was shaking her head, trying to smile at him.

'Oh no,' she said, in reply to his question, 'I am all right and quite comfortable here.'

But he still wondered what had caused her sudden pallor. However, he soon forgot about it, and when they parted for their mid-day meal it was already settled that they should meet there again in the afternoon and go up the Head.

'We need not go too far if you are tired,' he said, 'and we can have tea at the Eagle's Nest.'

The days which followed were like a dream to Nora. She and Harold Hastings met each day; in the mornings they would go for a swim, in the afternoons they went for walks or took the bus further afield to Kilmacanogue and its neighbourhood, and one never to be forgotten day they went to Glendalough. At night they went to the pictures, or more often just strolled talking along the Esplanade, listening to the band when it was playing. They flew past—those halcyon days—flew on winged feet. And each day Nora found herself more deeply in love with this man who had been unknown to her a week ago. She could hardly believe it. It all seemed incredible—absurd—that this should have happened to her. She who had never given a thought to a man before, and who had regarded herself as being absolutely impervious to any attractions from the opposite sex. Yet now, here she was with but one thought—one wish—counting the hours from one meeting to the next—happy only when with him. And she knew that he cared for her. Every look, every tone of his voice told her so, and she was inordinately happy that it should be so.

So happy was she that she entirely forgot for the time being the disgrace which overshadowed her life. It was strange that this should be so, she had always been so acutely conscious of the terrible fact—but so it was. Her new and totally unexpected happiness had caused her to forget all this. There was nothing in the world that mattered except just the wonder of Harold's love for her.

Two days before her leave was up, Harold had to go to Dublin on business, and did not get back until after seven that evening. The day seemed endless to Nora, and she found herself looking out for him long before he might be expected, although he had told her that he would be detained late owing to some legal case upon which Mr. Grey wished to have his advice.

'I'll have to have lunch with the old chap,' he said, 'and he will probably expect me to spend the afternoon with him, and you know I can't offend the old fellow—he has been too jolly decent to me.'

So after her mid-day meal in Mrs. Brennan's cottage, Nora took a book and sat down on the Esplanade. It was a lovely day and there was a band playing that afternoon. She had been sitting beside a lady for some time before she really noticed her. Her thoughts had wandered from the love story in her book to her own wonderful romance, and so she had been staring at the lady on the seat beside her without really seeing her at all. It was the lady's voice which brought her back to earth with a jerk.

'Well, my dear, if you have quite done staring at me, perhaps you will kindly withdraw your gaze and stare at someone else for a change.'

Nora flushed scarlet. 'Oh, I beg your pardon!' she said, 'I am so sorry—please forgive me! I was looking at you without knowing that I was doing so—indeed my thoughts were far away. I am really dreadfully sorry!'

The lady bent her head stiffly. 'I accept your apology,' she said, 'we will say no more about it.'

But now Nora found herself stealing glances at the speaker. She saw that she was very old. Her face was like a scroll of yellow parchment with a myriad of little lines finely drawn upon it; her eyes were faded and dim, yet she wore no glasses. Very little of her white hair could be seen under her old-fashioned bonnet. But it was her hands which held Nora's attention. She was gloveless—at least they were lying on her lap—and the hands were quite lovely, with their long, tapering fingers, so beautifully kept.

Summer Idyll

Nora, looking from the shabby attire of the old lady, could not help wondering about her. Who could she be? Certainly a lady—and a poor one.

As if in answer to her thoughts, the lady spoke again. 'I suppose you are here for your holidays?'

'Yes,' replied Nora, 'but I go back to work the day after tomorrow—worse luck,' with a rueful smile.

'A fortnight? That is a very short time,' remarked the other. 'However, the sort of people coming to Bray now do not stay for very long. In my young days they came for the season—taking a furnished house for several months.'

'They must have been fairly rich,' said Nora, 'to be able to afford a house—and for so long. I have only one room in a cottage.'

'Yes—they were certainly well to do,' was the reply; 'indeed only wealthy people could afford a Bray season in those days. The summer visitors then were a very different class from those we see now.'

As she was speaking a group of English working girls went past, arms linked so that they spread themselves across the width of the Esplanade, causing other people to move out of their way. They were singing—or rather shouting—in strident tones, 'She's a Lassie from Lancashire'. The old lady shuddered, as she glanced at them, and then averted her eyes quickly.

'How dreadful! she whispered.

'Yes, they are very vulgar,' agreed Nora. 'It is a pity they come here in such numbers—but of course they spend money in the town.' Then, after a moment, she remarked: 'I hope you don't mind the Dublin people coming here.'

'Certainly they are never so vulgar as that class,' replied the old lady, 'but still I must say that I do not like to see perambulators wheeled along the Esplanade.'

There was silence for a few moments, and then Nora made a remark about the band.

'Isn't the music good?' she said, 'I think that is the Number One Army Band.'

'It is not bad as bands go now,' was the reply; 'but we will never again hear music such as we had when the military were here.'

Nora stared at her. 'But this *is* a military band,' she said, puzzled.

The old lady stiffened. 'I am speaking of the British,' she said, curtly. 'I do not recognise these bands as being military. You should have heard the others, my dear, and you would know the difference.'

'I think these are all right,' replied the girl rather hotly, 'and I would not like to see either the British or their bands back again.'

The old lady looked angry and hurt. 'You cannot know what you are talking about,' she said. 'Look at the state of the country now.'

'Well, what about it?' asked Nora.

'It is heading for ruin,' was the reply. 'It is being ruled by the lower classes—the uneducated, and such people are never fit to govern. Why, there is hardly a good family left in Ireland—nearly all have gone to England or abroad. They have seen their estates divided up and given to their tenants—men who formerly worked under them. We have hardly anything left. Look at me—I who was Honoria Langdon of Langdon Court, near the Dargle—'

The old voice broke suddenly, but after a pause she went on: 'I don't know why I am telling you this, I never talk to strangers as a rule, but you have a nice face and I like you, although you are imbued with all these ridiculous new ideas—a democratic country, and so on. But it is no use to worry or lament over what is past and gone. Besides, I am over eighty now, and all my troubles will soon be over.'

Then, with a swift change of voice: 'Ah—here comes the dear Major!'

A dapper old gentleman was coming towards them, smart and straight in spite of his years, which must have been about the same as the old lady's. He swept off his hat with a flourish as he reached her side.

'My dear Miss Langdon,' he cried, 'it is surely time you returned to the house. You must be in great need of a cup of tea, and the Esplanade is so crowded with undesirable people that it is really no fit place for a lady. Let me have the honour of escorting you home.'

He held out his arm, and the old lady, with a little bow to Nora, placed her hand within it, and the curious couple—relics of a bygone age who might have stepped out of a Victorian album—walked away with mincing steps in the direction of the Meath Road.

Nora looked after them, amused, and yet sorry for them too.

'Two poor old things,' she thought, 'who have outlived their day. It must be sad to live as long as that and to have seen such changes all around them.'

She went home to her tea, and later when she met Harold Hastings and walked by his side, she forgot all about the old lady and the Major. She thought of nothing and of no one, save only the man at her side.

CHAPTER III

MARY GILFOYLE

None of us much enjoy our return to work after a holiday, and Nora was no exception to the rule. But in her case not only did she feel the usual distaste for the office routine, but she missed Harold Hastings more than she had thought it possible to do. There was a blank in her life which she now realised only he could fill.

There had been a change in the office staff even during the short time that she had been away. One of the girls had had an accident and fractured her arm, and the firm, while keeping her job open for her until she could return, had engaged another typist during her absence. Nora noticed this girl on the first morning she had gone back to work, and asked one of the others about her. There were four girls employed in the office, one as book-keeper, the others as shorthand typists. The business was good, the firm had a large connection all over the country, and the office was generally a busy place.

'Is May Kelly gone?' asked Nora in surprise, as she noticed the stranger seated in Miss Kelly's place.

'Yes,' replied Kitty Dunne, 'she had an accident, her arm. It's a wonder she was not killed. Miss Gilfoyle is here until she returns, I must introduce you. Miss Malcolm—this is Miss Gilfoyle.'

The new girl glanced up from her typewriter and Nora found herself looking into a pair of honest grey eyes, set in an intelligent, open countenance.

'Not at all pretty,' she thought to herself. But someway she was sure that it was a face to be trusted.

'Nora has been away on her holidays for the past fortnight,' explained Kitty Dunne. 'I am sure,' she added, with a laugh, 'that you two will be friends—you are both so serious-minded and so quiet.'

This was certainly more than Kitty herself could claim to be, she was the gayest and most pleasure-loving of mortals. And yet very lovable and with no real harm in her.

Nora, too, thought that she would like this new girl, but for the first few days they only exchanged a few remarks. Nora, in fact, was too full of her own affairs. Her one joy at this time was receiving a letter from Harold Hastings. He had written several times, saying how much he missed her, adding that he was tired of Bray and did not think that he would stay there for the remainder of his month's holiday. He had said nothing definite to her when they parted, but both knew that their friendship was not of the usual ephemeral kind—past and forgotten when the holidays were over. Nora knew that she cared for him, and the man guessed that she was far from indifferent towards him. She had given him her address in Rathmines, and now she lived for his letters. This girl, who had never troubled herself about any man, had now fallen deeply and irrevocably in love. Her romance coloured all her days; except when she was actually at work she thought of nothing else, and even when her typewriter was busily clicking away answering letters from farmers and shopkeepers all over the country, one part of her was walking along the roads around Bray by the side of Harold Hastings. On the office staff besides Kitty Dunne and the new girl, there was Rose Malone. She was a tall, handsome woman, rather older than the others. She posed as being of the ultra-modern type, spending most of her evenings at various dance halls in the company of one of the young men, of whom, according to her own story, she had a plentiful number, only anxious to act as her escort. This girl was rather free in her talk, and was not averse to telling some 'smutty' stories. Nora had always ignored her, she had no interest in such conversation which simply disgusted and bored her, but she had been sorry to see that the other two girls—both a good deal younger than Rose Malone—laughed a little at these stories, and even if they did not like them, had not the courage to say so to one who was so much their senior in the office.

But it was a very different in the case of Mary Gilfoyle. The very first occasion upon which Rose told one of these stories, she looked up from her typewriter, and said, quietly: 'I must ask you not to repeat this kind of story in the office, Miss Malone. They are not fit for young girls to hear—nor, indeed, any decent woman.' Rose stared at her with angry surprise—she could hardly believe her ears. 'Well, she said, 'if this is not cheek! I would ask you to kindly remember, Miss Gilfoyle, that you are the junior in this office—and only temporary at that. As for me, I shall tell what stories I like, and I don't care a damn for you or your sanctimonious airs.'

This occurred two days after Nora's return to the office, and she now paused in her work—as did the others—to listen to the reply from Miss Gilfoyle. It came at once in a quiet voice, not raised by a tone, unlike that of Rose, which had been decidedly shrill.

'But I do not think that you will do so,' she said. 'I should hate to have to report the matter to Mr. Murphy , but rather than have these young girls contaminated by the conversation of an older woman who should know better, I shall be compelled to do so.'

Rose Malone stared at her, speechless from anger and surprise. She had never expected this, and she knew that Mr. Murphy was a very strict man, a devout Catholic and a Legionary, one who would never for one moment have allowed such conversations to be held in his office. He was a kind and just employer and they all liked and respected him, with the exception of Rose, who called him—behind his back—a 'sanctimonious old prig'. Never for one instant had she thought that this new girl—and a temporary one at that!—would have dared to act in such a manner. But Rose realised that Mary Gilfoyle meant what she said, and she could not risk this coming to the ears of 'old Murphy', so muttering a few remarks about sneaks and tale-bearers, she said no more and went on with her work in silence.

The others were as surprised as Rose herself, but from that day they regarded Mary Gilfoyle with respect. They had not liked those dirty stores which Rose had retailed with her air of a woman of the modern world, but they had been too much afraid of her to object openly. Nora, as we have said, had simply ignored both the woman and her stories. But now here was someone who was not afraid of Rose, who was brave enough to stand up to her, and had been able to stop her from telling any more dirty stories or jokes. They were decent girls, and they were glad that this had happened. And such a quiet girl, too. Nora glanced at her, sitting there quite unconcerned, going on steadily with her work and apparently unconscious of the bombshell which she had flung that day into the office of Messrs. Murphy and Co.

Kitty Dunne spoke to Mary Gilfoyle later.

'I'm glad you stood up to Rose,' she said. 'May Kelly and myself did not like her stories, but to tell you the truth, we were afraid of her. She was here a good while before us, and Mr. Murphy thinks a lot of her. Of course he hasn't the least idea of the way she goes on—she is always so sweet and good, quite the saint—when he is around. But she is a real cat, and if I were you I should mind myself from now on, for she is sure to have her knife in you.'

'I am not afraid of her,' was the quiet reply, 'and I would not dream of listening to that kind of talk without a protest. I think it is very wrong that she should be allowed to repeat such things before you girls—for she is a good deal older than any of you.'

'All the same—beware of her,' said Kitty, but then she added: 'However, as you are only temporary here, it will not matter much to you—she can do little to injure you.'

But very soon it became known that May Kelly was not returning to the office. She had been engaged for some months to a young fellow in the National Army, and as he had just got his Captaincy, he wished to get married as soon as May was all right again, for he did not want her to go back to the office. So as Mary Gilfoyle had given every satisfaction in her work Mr. Murphy asked her to take Miss Kelly's place. Kitty Dunne and Nora were very glad, they both liked this quiet, dignified girl who was so pleasant to work with in every way. The only one who resented her appointment was Miss Malone, and she seemed to have conceived a very real dislike to Mary. Ever since that morning when the 'sneak' as she called her—had spoken to her, quietly, yet firmly, Rose had done everything possible to annoy her in little ways, but, to her chagrin, Mary Gilfoyle seemed utterly unconscious of it all. She, like Nora, simply ignored Rose and so they both earned that lady's dislike—to use no stronger expression.

If Nora had not been so absolutely absorbed in her thoughts of Harold Hastings at this time, it is likely that she and Mary would have become fast friends, but to Nora at the moment there was only one individual in the whole world who mattered. She thought of him by day, dreamt of him by night, and when she received a letter telling her that he had left Bray and returned to Dublin, and asking her to meet him that evening, the whole horizon was rose-tinted for her.

That was the beginning of weeks of happiness. On week evenings they would meet for tea somewhere after the office, and then either cycle or go for a bus ride to the sea or country. At the week-end it was the same, hours of happiness were spent by them in one or other of Dublin's beauty spots. So happy was she at times that Nora grew almost frightened. Surely this was too wonderful to be true—too beautiful to last.

And all this time, the remembrance of her father's tragedy stayed in the background. She simply refused to think about it. Later, she would have to tell Harold. But, after all, he had not yet spoken, they were just friends—great friends—but no more. Yet in her heart, she knew that it was only a matter of time—and perhaps not very long—before he told her that he loved her—wanted her for his wife. And then she supposed she would have to speak, it would not be possible for her to keep her future husband in ignorance of the terrible tragedy which had clouded all her life—he would have a right to know.

But it would be time enough later on to think seriously of these things. Let this glorious summer continue, let her sail these halcyon seas while she could do so, living in each golden hour—forgetting all else but her happiness.

It was one Sunday in August when Harold spoke to her. They were sitting on the slope of Tibradden Mountain, having cycled there early in the afternoon. They had brought their tea with them and had enjoyed boiling the little kettle on the fire of dry sticks. Harold had carried the kettle and the tea, but Nora had provided the eatables. Each had their own cup and spoon. They were eating sandwiches and cake and found it delightful.

'This is better than Mrs. Dwyer's Sunday dinner of tough beef and cabbage, of which I partook before I came out,' remarked Harold. 'I hope your landlady does you better?' he added.

'Oh, I look after myself,' replied Nora.

'How on earth do you manage that?'

'Well, it's easy enough these hot days. I take a light lunch in town and then have something with my tea in the evening. Generally a salad does me—I don't care much for meat in the summer.' She laughed gaily as she poured out the tea, and added, 'I would rather have a meal like this—it is such fun!'

'Yes, and the sandwiches are grand,' said Harold. 'I tried to get on the soft side of Mrs. Dwyer, but she said she had something else to do besides making sandwiches for the boarders. Our tea was there for us if we liked to come home for it, but she wasn't supposed to provide tea to be eaten out of the house.'

'What a horrid woman she must be!' said Nora.

'Not at all—just the usual landlady type. A friend of mine stayed once at a place where the landlady was unique, she spoilt her boarders—would make them up packets of sandwiches, and so on, if they were going anywhere. Of course most of the fellows played on her, and she lost a lot of money. But she was not the stuff of which the usual landlady is made. I say—this is great cake—where did you buy it?'

'Nowhere—I made it myself.'

'Well—you *are* a fine cook and no mistake—it's a pleasure to get a home-made cake like this.'

As they were finishing their tea a very thin, hungry-looking collie dog approached, eyeing the food with wistful looks.

'You poor thing!' cried Nora. 'Have a bit of cake.'

The dog wolfed it down in a second.

'Oh, he is starving! she exclaimed, supplying him with the remains of the sandwiches. 'Yes,' said Harold. 'It's a pity, but the people who own these dogs do not feed them very well, and they are such fine animals. But their owners as a rule look upon them as slaves and seldom show them any friendliness or kindness, yet no dog is so faithful as a collie. Some friends of mine near Kilmacanogue knew people who owned one, a grand animal and very faithful. He worked hard for them, and on one occasion saved the lives of two lambs, staying out all night on the mountain and bringing them safely home at last. Yet when the poor beast got old and was no longer any good for work his owners were going to put an end to his life by hanging. My friends, who are great animal lovers, took pity on the dog and brought him to their own home, where he spent the rest of his life in such comfort as he had never known before.'

'It's good to know that,' said Nora. 'I often think how strange it is that we Irish are so cruel to our animals—because we certainly are. People treat their horses and dogs—and the poor little donkeys—with great cruelty sometimes.'

'You are right—and this poor fellow is thin enough anyway.'

They gave him the remainder of their meal, and then when he saw there was no more food about, he went off giving a wag of a rather drooping tail as it to say 'Thank you.'

They put away the things in their basket and then sat quietly enjoying the peace and loveliness which was all around them. There was not a soul in sight, any Sunday hikers had gone further afield to the top of the hill, and these two were alone. They seemed to be alone in the whole world. No sounds were to be heard but the notes of the birds, and the distant lowing of cattle. A sudden silence had fallen between them. It was broken by Harold.

'Nora,' he said. She turned and looked at him, and what she saw in his eyes made her lower her own.

'Nora,' he said again. 'I think you know what I want to say—don't you? I love you—I have loved you from the first day when we met in the rain on Bray Head. Do you care for me at all? Will you marry me?'

CHAPTER IV

THE SHADOW FROM THE PAST

For a moment Nora did not speak—she could not do so. Rather nervous, Harold looked at her.

'Nora—answer me. Don't keep me in suspense. Do you care for me at all?'

She only lifted her eyes and looked at him—and he read his answer there. It was a little while before they came down to earth and were able to talk of mundane things. Then Harold told her that Mr. Grey had spoken to him a few days ago, saying that he intended making him a partner at the beginning of the coming year. 'So that decided me,' he said.

'Consideration of the financial aspect had been rather worrying me, but now that will be all right. You see, I have my mother to help. As you know, she lives with her sister in Wexford. My aunt has a small annuity, but I like to send them what help I can. My dear mother has had so much trouble, she has suffered so much, that I feel that I can never do enough for her.'

He paused for a moment and then went on, rather reluctantly, as it seemed to Nora. 'My father was well off—quite a wealthy man—but he lost his money—through no fault of his own—and mother and myself were left badly off. Mr. Grey was a great friend of the family, and I have a lot to thank him for. He helped us a lot, and when it was necessary for me to get work as soon as possible, he took me as clerk into his office. Afterwards, too, he helped me with my examination fees, and so on. I owe him more than I can ever repay.'

'He must be a dear,' said Nora. Then, after a pause, she asked, rather nervously: 'Does—does your mother know about me?'

Harold smiled at her. 'Yes,' he replied, 'Mum and myself have no secrets from each other. You are to come soon to Wexford and be introduced to her.'

Nora flushed. 'Oh—I hope she will like me. Do you thing she will?'

'Of course she will. She likes what I like—and who could resist you—my little quiet bird?'

They sat in silence for a while, content and happy. Then Harold asked a question which made Nora's happiness take frightened wings and fly away for the moment.

'Your parents are dead, are they not?' And as Nora nodded dumbly, he added, 'I am always so sorry for anyone who has not a mother. I was fond of my dad, too, but mother always came first, and that is why——'

He stopped speaking suddenly and Nora glanced at him in surprise. He seemed for the moment to have forgotten her, and so stern had his expression become that he looked older than his real age.

'How old are you, Harold?' she asked. He was his smiling self again, as he replied, 'Oh, I am twenty-four—nearly twenty-five. I was twenty-one when dad died—and that was three years ago.'

Three years ago. That was when her own tragedy had happened. Strange that they should have suffered at the same time. And that brought to her mind the realisation that she must tell Harold all about it. But not just now—not today when such perfect happiness was hers. No—she would wait for another time when they were discussing matters in a more sensible manner—not uplifted, as they were now, on the wings of love in the seventh heaven. Yet his next question brought more uneasiness to her mind.

'Won't you tell me a little about your people?' he asked, 'you have never told me anything.'

She felt herself go still and cold and hoped that he would not notice it, sitting there in the sunlight, with his arm around her. And yet was the sun really shining? Or was it growing dark and cold? As she did not speak, Harold went on: 'Of course you told me that your parents were dead. Are you quite alone in the world? No brothers or sisters or other relatives?'

'No—I am an only child.'

'And your parents—are they long dead?'

'Three years.'

'Three years? Just as long as my dear father. But I have my mother still alive, thank God. But you are not so fortunate. Did your father die first?'

'Yes.'

'And did your mother live for long afterwards?'

Nora moistened her tongue which was gone dry.

Would he never cease this cross-examination?

'No,' she replied then, 'there was but a few weeks between them.'

He waited, expecting her to give him further details, but she remained silent. He glanced at her rather curiously. How strangely reticent she was!

Still it might well be that she had felt her loss so much that she did not care to talk about it. Yet to him—her future husband surely——?

However, Harold was not one to pursue a subject when he saw that it was not congenial to the girl. No doubt she had her own reasons; no doubt, also, she would soon tell him all about her people. Nora was a shy sort of little person and might wish to wait until later before telling him her family history—not that he supposed there was much to tell.

'Well, I suppose we had better get a move on,' he said, 'everything is safely packed on the carriers.'

They made their way down the mountain side rather silently. At their feet was the city, looking like a dream city, sleeping there in the light of the setting sun. Up there, where they were, the noises of the modern city could not be heard—the clang of trams or the roaring of motor cars. Dublin lay beneath them, like a picture on an easel. The sight of it aroused Nora from her morbid reflections, and she became happy again. Time enough to worry over the past later on when she had to confide her story to Harold. Why torment herself now and spoil this heavenly evening?

'How lovely Dublin is!' she murmured softly. 'Do you know those lines that Hugh MacCartan wrote?'

> 'Nature has clothed Thee with sovereignty,
> Robed Thee with purple of the heather hills
> Yellow of gorse, silver of mountain rills,
> And for Thy footstool made the emerald sea.'

'Yes–I know them well,' he replied 'in fact I think I know nearly every poem that was ever written about Dublin. I read one once supposed to be written by an old man—and perhaps it was, for all I know. It shows the love of Dublin all through the man's life. Listen—

> 'The shining hills of Dublin
>   That guard her smiling plain,
> That beckon to the wanderer
>   And lure the dreamy swain;
> How oft alone in freedom
>   I climbed their verdant slopes
> With step full strong and strident,
>   And youth's fond dreams and hopes.

>   The shining hills of Dublin
>   Still heard my manhood's tread,
>   Though years had touched me gently
>   In passing o'er my head.
>   But there was one beside me
>   To echo all my joy,
>   To reflect dreams of boyhood,
>   My friend, my son, my boy.
>
>   The shining hills of Dublin
>   Are now for me no more,
>   My step is slow and feeble,
>   My heart is full and sore.
>   But you, my boy, will climb them.
>   And though alone you be,
>   You'll sing their praise hereafter
>   In memory of me.'

'That is lovely,' said Nora, 'and after all there is no city like it. I think that we Dubliners do not half appreciate our city—we simply take it for granted.'

So talking they sped down the hills, through Whitechurch, and were soon in Rathfarnham, and shortly afterwards had reached Rathmines and Nora's abode. Harold said goodbye to her, and the next moment she was wheeling her bicycle up the little garden path before the house.

As she entered and stepped into the hall, the familiar odour of boiled cabbage assailed her nostrils. It was queer, she often thought, that this same odour was seldom absent, yet Mrs. Doyle could not always be boiling cabbage—or could she? The landlady now appeared at the top of the stairs leading to the basement, which was her own special domain and where she lived and slept.

'Oh, it's you, Miss Malcolm. I thought it might be Pat's wife—she's not back yet from Merrion, and the Lord knows it's too late to have those children out.'

'Oh, it's a lovely evening, Mrs. Doyle—and quite warm. They will be all right,' said Nora as she passed into her room, after first putting her bicycle away in a small recess at the end of the hall.

Mrs. Doyle was a small, sharp-featured little woman. She was not really ill-natured, but generations of lodgers had soured the milk of human kindness within her breast. Her life was a constant struggle

The Shadow from the Past 29

to make ends meet, so that her face wore a perpetual expression of anxiety. The house was of fair size, and was now full. Nora's room was on the right of the hall, a good-sized room, furnished as a bed-sittingroom; the room opposite was occupied by a widow of 'independent means,' of whom Mrs. Doyle thought very highly. Upstairs were Mrs. Doyle's married son and his wife and two children—'Pat's wife', of whom she had spoken to Nora, and between whom and herself a perpetual feud reigned. In another room was her unmarried son, a tall, goodlooking young man, lazy and easy-going, who lived more or less on his mother. Needless to say, she adored him, nothing that George did could be wrong, and she seemed to believe all his cock-and-bull stories about looking for work. He resembled her late husband in appearance, and Nora often thought that the late lamented must have been rather like his son in other ways, too. The married son, on the contrary, was the replica of his mother, small and dark. He was a hard-working little man, and besides paying rent regularly to his mother, often helped her in other ways as well. But Mrs. Doyle looked upon him as inferior in every way to her handsome George.

Yet another lodger—or tenant, as the landlady preferred to call them—was little Miss Moran, an elderly spinster, living on a tiny income and wholly devoted to a tiny Yorkshire terrier.

Nora had managed to make her room fairly comfortable; she had a few personal belongings from the old home of happier days, her books, some good china—even a few silver spoons which had been saved from the wreck. They had been bought at the auction by her friends, the Derwents, and given to her.

She was suddenly very tired, but she did not feel sleepy and sat down by the open window to think. But her thoughts went round and round, in a vicious circle, always coming back to the same point. She must tell Harold about her father, and then would arise the question: How would he take it? Would he be so horrified, so disgusted, that he would resolve to have nothing more to do with her? She knew that many a man would think twice before taking a wife whose father had been a thief and a suicide. On the other hand, if Harold really loved her, would he not overlook all that? After all she was herself—not her father. Of course she knew that there was the factor of heredity to think about, and it counted for much. But it had been trouble and worry which had driven her father to distraction. Such a thing had often happened to others.

And was she to be blamed for it anyhow? Yes, she would tell Harold—tell him soon and get it over. Then she would be at peace and happy. But not yet—not just yet. She would wait just a little while. There could be no harm in letting these few days pass—such happy, happy days!—before she told him.

Yet when the clock in the Rathmines Town Hall struck three she was still lying awake still worrying, her thoughts going round and round in her head, and her body tossing from side to side, restless and sleepless. And she heard the quarters ring out for four o'clock before at last she fell into a troubled sleep.

CHAPTER V

LILAC TREE HOUSE

It was only a cottage really, although designated by the name of 'House'. A delightful cottage all the same, with a warm, thatched roof, an old-fashioned garden, and diamond-paned windows. It was situated a little way beyond Whitechurch, near the mountains, but in a sheltered spot, so that, even in winter, those who lived there did not feel the cold winds which blew sometimes so fiercely down the mountain side.

But on this warm evening in August, it was like a fairy cottage, the sun shining on thatch and gable and the scent of the flowers meeting one at the gate. A lady sat sewing in the porch, middle-aged, with a sweet, rather worn face. She seemed one who had met with sorrow and supped with him by the way. Her hair was snow white. Presently she raised her head to listen. She had heard the familiar sound of the bus arriving from the city, and it was generally about the same time that her daughter also arrived cycling home from her work. Very shortly the click of the garden gate announced her arrival, and she came up the path, wheeling her bicycle. Stooping to kiss her mother, she asked: 'Well, motherkin—how are you? Did you get the day fairly well?'

Mrs. Gilfoyle was not strong, being more or less crippled with rheumatism, and it was with difficulty that she got around. Still, she seldom complained

The cottage consisted of five rooms, including the kitchen. There were three bedrooms and a sittingroom—the old-fashioned word 'parlour' would have suited it better. Low-ceilinged, with cupboards built into the wall, it was furnished with several bits of good old furniture. Old prints were on the walls, a china cupboard was in one corner, and there was a well-stocked bookcase.

It was here in the summer that Mrs. Gilfoyle and her two daughters had their meals—except breakfast, which they took in the kitchen, as Mary had not much time, having to cycle into the city and be at her employment at nine.

'Is that you, Mary?' called a voice from the kitchen, 'your tea is just ready.'

'All right—I am ready for it, too—I just want to wash my face and hands. I am so hot and dusty.'

Soon the family were seated at the table, the roses nodding in through the open casement. Mary had some cold meat and salad, in her lunch hour she only had a modest meal—generally tea and scones—so she was ready for her tea and enjoyed it.

Anne, the elder girl, did not go to business, she had no aptitude for it. She stayed at home, where indeed she was wanted, looked after the house and her mother, attended to the garden and poultry, and was never idle.

'Well, how are things in the office?' she now asked Mary. 'How is the charming Rose? Any more kind attentions from her?'

'Not more than usual. Besides, I don't mind her—I can look after myself,' replied Mary. 'But,' she added, 'I am a bit anxious about that nice girl I told you about.'

'Nora Malcolm? But I thought she ignored Miss Malone?'

'So she does—but Rose does not ignore her, and I fear she will yet find a way to revenge herself upon the girl. She is such a nice little thing, too. I wish I knew her better, but she is so reserved. Of late, too, she seems to have something on her mind—she is certainly worried about something.'

'Why not ask her out here some Sunday?'

'I don't think she would come. As a matter of fact, I rather fancy that there is a young man about; if so I hope that things are going all right for her. She seems quite alone in the world.'

'Oh, then you should certainly ask her here, and let mother talk to her,' said Anne.

'Yes, ask her by all means,' said Mrs. Gilfoyle, 'she can only refuse.'

And Mary did ask Nora—and much to her surprise the invitation was accepted. The reason for this—which naturally Mary did not know—was the fact that Harold would be absent from Dublin for the coming week-end. He had had to go to Cork on some important legal business for Mr. Grey and had told Nora that he would not be back in Dublin before the Tuesday of the next week. So as she knew that she would be terribly lonely without him, she agreed to visit Lilac Tree House and have tea there on the Sunday afternoon. It would keep her from brooding and worrying over the past—so at least she had thought.

Mary was waiting for her where the bus stopped at the end of the road on which stood Lilac Tree House. When Nora saw the cottage she gave a little cry of delighted surprise.

Lilac Tree House

'Oh—what a lovely place! Is this where you live, Miss Gilfoyle?'

'Yes,' replied the other. Adding: 'And now I hope you will call me Mary, as I hope we are going to be good friends.'

'I hope so, too, Mary,' replied Nora, rather shyly, as they walked up the path to the house.

Mrs. Gilfoyle was sitting in the porch, reading. She was watching the girls coming up the path, and as they came near she dropped her book and rose to her feet. 'Why—Nora Tiernan—is it really *you?*' she cried.

Nora, now as white as a sheet, looked at her speechless, aghast.

'You remember me surely?' went on Mrs. Gilfoyle, 'your mother was my near neighbour when we lived at Rathgar.'

Still no word from Nora, only that frozen, almost terrified look.

Mary, who saw that something was wrong, now interposed, in her quiet voice. 'You must be mistaken, mother. This is the friend we were expecting—Miss Malcolm, from the office.'

Mrs. Gilfoyle did not speak at once, she was staring at Nora's white face. Then she said, her voice as controlled and quiet as her daughter's: 'I beg your pardon, Miss Malcolm, for my mistake, but you are very like someone I knew a few years ago. Please forgive me—my sight is not very good. And now come inside, you must be tired after the bus—it is so hot.'

Nora, without speaking, went with them into the house. Her mind was in a perfect turmoil. So here was Mrs. Gilfoyle, whom she remembered coming often to see her mother at their house in Rathgar. She faintly recalled to mind that Mr. Gilfoyle had died and soon afterwards the family had gone to live in a house, which had been left them by an old aunt, some miles outside the city. How stupid she had been not to have remembered this when she had met Mary. But then, she had never known either Mary or her sister when their parents lived in Rathgar. Both the girls had been in Belgium for several years, living with a cousin there. When their father had died, and their mother's health declined, they had returned to Ireland and all had gone to live near Whitechurch. Nora had never connected the Mary Gilfoyle, whom she had met in the office, with the Gilfoyles of Rathgar. She had long ago forgotten all about those people and so had never dreamt of such a chance meeting as this which had just taken place. She wondered that Mrs. Gilfoyle had remembered her so well. It was such a long time since they had met—it must be five years, and she—Nora—had been only sixteen. She forgot that to a woman of Mrs. Gilfoyle's age five years is a short time, and she had recognised Nora at once, for hers was no ordinary face.

Nora's visit to Lilac Tree House could not be called a success after this. She tried to talk and to behave naturally, but it was not possible. All the while she was thinking that now Mary Gilfoyle would know all about her—because, of course, her mother would be sure to tell her. Would Mary tell the other girls in the office? How Rose would sneer at her. And would she be able to keep her position once Mr. Murphy knew about her father? Nora could not forget the rebuffs with which she had met before she had changed her name. She could hardly swallow a mouthful of delicious homemade bread and cakes which Anne had so carefully prepared, she just felt as if every mouthful would choke her, and she was glad indeed when the evening drew to a close.

'I am sure Miss Malcolm would like some flowers to take back with her,' said Mrs. Gilfoyle, 'so will you gather them for her, Mary; and you, Anne might get her some eggs—I expect it is not easy to get new-laid ones in the city. Miss Malcolm and myself will sit in the porch and wait for you—but don't be long, for she must not miss her bus.'

When they were alone, Mrs. Gilfoyle was silent for a few moments. Nora, wondering what she was going to say, glanced rather timidly at her, but the older woman only said, quietly, 'I just wanted you to know, my dear, that your secret is safe with me. You no doubt know best the reason why you have changed your name. I do not wish to be curious—it is entirely your own business, and I will speak to no one about the matter.'

Nora murmured 'Thank you,' through trembling lips. She might have said more, but there was no time, as Mary came with the flowers.

'I hear the bus,' she cried. 'You must go, Nora, it wouldn't do to miss it—the next one is very late and always crowded.'

The next moment goodbyes were being said, and Nora was speeding quickly down the road. Mary went with her to the bus. She was puzzled, and hoped that Nora would say something to her. But the other girl only thanked her for the pleasant evening she had spent, while thinking to herself what a travesty those thanks were, and hoping that she would never see Lilac Tree House again. Then she was in the bus on her way citywards.

'What on earth is the matter, mother?' asked Anne.

'Yes—what does it mean at all?' asked Mary.

'Did you know Nora Malcolm before? And why did you call her Nora Tiernan?'

'I cannot tell you,' replied Mrs. Gilfoyle.

'But surely you can tell us where you met her before? How you came to know her?'

'No—I cannot.'

'You mean you will not?'

'Well, then, I will not. I do know the girl—knew her when you both were in Belgium before your dear father died, but she wishes that what I know will be kept a secret. I am in honour bound to respect her wishes in this matter.'

'Then you will tell us nothing?' said Mary.

'I will tell you nothing. Indeed, I wonder that you girls should ask me. Miss Malcolm has been our guest, and it would be strange indeed if I were to go against her wishes.'

Her daughters were disappointed—especially Mary, who could not help being curious. Not that her curiosity was of the usual vulgar type—she was not that kind of girl. But she liked Nora, and of late, as she told her mother, she had been anxious about her and would have liked to be able to help her were she in any sort of trouble. And now, her mother knew something about her, and yet she would not tell. Mary could not understand it at all.

Anne did not mind so much. Nora was a stranger to her, and although she wondered what her secret could be, she did not worry about it. Besides, both the girls knew that once their mother had spoken there was an end of the matter. She would say no more about it.

But Mary lay awake for some time that night, wondering and wondering what it could all mean.

There was another who lay awake that night—and for longer than Mary, and that was Nora herself. She had been so careful, as she thought, to bury Nora Tiernan and become Nora Malcolm. She had been so sure that she had covered all her tracks. And now here was someone who recognised her, someone whose daughter worked in the same office with Nora herself. Poor Nora, she had gone through such a terrible time of humiliation when first looking for work that she could never forget it. Yet it was not the fear of losing her job which kept her wakeful through all the weary hours of that night. She felt fairly certain that Mr. Murphy, who was such an eminently just and kind man, would not now dismiss her after two years' of good service just because of her father. No—that was not the fear that gripped her by the throat, causing sleep to fly far from her. It was the thought of Harold Hastings.

Yet had she not long ago made up her mind to tell? She had really meant to do so, but somehow of late her resolution had faded. Constantly putting off the telling of it, had made her resolution waver, until lately she had found herself asking the question as to whether it was really necessary to tell Harold about her father's tragedy. In her sober senses she would have acknowledged that such a step was undoubtedly the right and proper one to take—the only honourable thing to do. But her love for Harold made her fearful and afraid. Suppose that when he heard her story he should turn away from her? Tell her that he could not marry the daughter of a suicide and a thief? She might lose him for ever, and she could not bear that—it would kill her. She loved him so much. Never had she loved anyone so much—never would she love anyone in the same way.

But if they were once married—if she were his wife—then even if he heard the story either from her own lips or by some other means—surely he would not turn against her then. Or would he feel even more bitter about it?

She tossed and turned all the night through, unable to make up her mind one way or another, while all the time deadly fear lay upon her. Had she herself been the guilty one, she could not have suffered more. Surely if those who—like John Tiernan—take 'the coward's way out'—if they could but realise what misery and shame they are storing up for those they leave behind—they would think twice before acting in such a manner.

Nora went into the office on the Monday morning, looking so pale and weary that Rose Malone remarked, sneeringly: 'Are you not well, Miss Malcolm? I am afraid you could not have had a very happy week-end.'

Nora brought her pride to her aid.

'I had a most enjoyable time, thank you,' she replied. 'I had tea yesterday with Miss Gilfoyle and her mother and sister at their lovely house near Whitechurch.'

Miss Malone gave a contemptuous sniff. 'Well, I can't say that you look much the better for it,' she replied.'Was the boy friend not there?'

Nora sat down at her machine without replying, but for the first time her heart beat with sudden fear and not joy when she thought of Harold Hastings.

CHAPTER VI
MARGARET CONROY

Mrs. Hastings and her sister, Miss Annabella Martin, lived together in a small cottage some two miles outside the town of Wexford. Miss Martin was a frail little woman of sixty-five, who had spent most of her life as companion to various ladies, mostly of the semi-invalid type. None of them seemed very grateful to Miss Martin for bearing with their whims and fancies, and hers had been a hard life until she had gone to live with her last employer. Mrs. Reid was a kind woman, and when she died had left a sum of money to buy a small annuity for 'Annabella Martin, my faithful companion and friend for the past seven years.' It had been a godsend to Miss Martin, and she had gladly retired from being a companion to strangers and had settled down in this cottage of four rooms with its bit of garden. When her sister had lost her husband under such tragic circumstances, she had been only too delighted to have her company. They lived quite happily together, seldom having any differences of opinion, and both having one person in common whom they adored—Harold, the son of one, the nephew of the other. And they had reason to love him. He had been a good son and a kind nephew. Even when he had first started to work, and his salary had been small, he had always managed to send something to these two to whom he was really attached. Of late he had been able to very materially supplement their rather slender resources. But now that would be all changed, for even if he were to be made partner soon, he would not be able to help them very much—nor would it be right for him to do so, or for them to expect it—Harold had told them that he had met the one girl in the world for him, and she had promised to marry him at the beginning of the coming year—and they were now in September.

Their modest mid-day meal was finished, everything tidied and put away, the cottage, as usual, a picture of neatness and order, and they had taken a book and some sewing into the tiny garden at the side of the house. There was one apple tree there—the pride of Miss Martin's heart—and there they brought their seats and sat down on this golden September afternoon. It was Annabella's custom to read aloud while her sister sewed. But the book did not appear to be interesting and was presently put aside, while the sisters began to talk of that which was just then nearest to their heart, and so, for the hundredth time, Mrs. Hastings remarked: I wonder what she is like, Annabella?'

'Well, Harold tells us that she is everything that is lovely,' replied her sister, 'but of course we must take his opinion with a grain of salt.'

'I suppose so. Still, I don't think he would have fallen in love with a girl who wasn't—well, rather nice.'

'No—I don't think so either,' replied her sister, 'but one never knows with men. Love blinds them.'

Then, after a pause, she added: 'I feel rather sorry about Margaret Conroy. I always hoped that she and Harold would make a match of it.'

'I hoped so too,' said Mrs. Hastings, 'but I suppose it was not to be. And perhaps when we meet this other girl, we shall like her too.'

'Perhaps. But she will never be like Margaret to me.'

'Nor to me,' replied Mrs. Hastings.

At that moment the click of the gate leading into the garden was heard, and looking up, Miss Martin exclaimed: 'Talk of angels—here is Margaret!'

'So it is,' said her sister. Adding: 'She does not know yet—shall we tell her?'

'Well, I'm afraid we had better. Let me do it, Ellen, I think I can manage it better than you.'

Both watched the girl now advancing along the little path towards them—and she was well worth looking at, was Margaret Conroy, on that day in September. She was tall and slender, with clear-cut features, and a colour in her cheeks which was Nature's own—and not bought in a shop. Her blue-black hair was loosely knotted at the back of her neck, and her dark eyes were smiling as well as her lips as she called out: 'Well—you dears—how are you at all?'

They smiled in return, in spite of the anxiety which they were feeling just at the moment. Somehow, one had always to smile with Margaret. Happiness seemed to radiate from her—happiness and contentment. Yet some people would have said that she had little to be happy about. She lived with her great-grandfather, a man over ninety, who had seen his son, and his son's son, pass into the Great Beyond, while he was still left behind. A wonderful old man for his age, still hale and hearty, and able even to help with the work on his small farm. He often told his great-grandson—Margaret's brother, Patrick—that he knew more about farming than *he* did—

in spite of all the new-fangled notions taught to farmers nowadays. At times he was cross-grained and difficult to put up with. Patrick often lost patience with him, but Margaret could nearly always manage him.

'Faith, but ould Conroy is a mortal terror—so he is!' was the verdict of all the neighbourhood. Yet there was many a one who had been glad of his advice and help in times past—and some who still sought it.

'Come and sit down, dear,' said Mrs. Hastings. 'Did you walk over?'

'Oh, no—I have my bike—I left it at the door. She seated herself on the grass at their feet. 'What a lovely day!' she said, 'just golden! That is the only word to discribe these early autumn days when summer still lingers. I don't think one could be anything but happy on such a day.'

The eyes of the other two met across her dark head, but they did not speak.

'Any letter from Harold since I saw you last?' asked Margaret.

'Yes—we had one yesterday.'

'An special news?'

Miss Martin spoke then. 'He is coming down at the week-end,' she said.

'How nice. It seems a long time since he was here,' said Margaret.

The old ladies were silent. What could they say? Unconsciously the girl was making it harder for them to speak. But Annabella knew that it would be better to get it over as soon as possible.

'He is not coming alone this time,' she said.

'No? Who is he bringing with him? Not the great Mr. Grey himself?'

'No.'

For the life of her, Miss Martin could not go on. Her instinct told her that she was about to shatter, with one blow, the happiness of this girl, sitting there on the grass so absolutely unconscious of what she was about to hear.

'No—not Mr. Grey,' she said, and stopped.

'Then who?' asked Margaret, 'it must be someone very important, you are both looking so solemn!'

Mrs. Hastings, sitting so quietly, gave the girl a quick glance, but it was quite obvious that Margaret had not the faintest idea of what she was to hear. Annabella spoke then.

'He is bringing the girl he is going to marry,' she said, 'he wants us to know her.'

There was no word from the girl at their feet. They could not see her face and she made no movement, only sat perfectly still. Mrs. Hastings, feeling the silence acutely, rushed quickly into speech.

'We have not met her yet, and know little about her, so we shall be anxious to make her acquaintance.'

'They are to arrive on Saturday afternoon by the bus,' said Miss Martin. 'The girl works as typist in an office—some big seed merchants, I believe.'

Rather doubtfully, she went on: 'We were hoping you might cycle over and join us at tea—or later in the evening. Could you come?'

Then Margaret spoke, but she still kept her face averted.

'Thanks very much,' she said, 'I should have been delighted, but I have promised to have tea with Eileen Madigan on Saturday— she has not been too well.'

'Oh, well—we shall see you at Mass on Sunday,' said Mrs. Hastings.

'Yes—I expect so.'

As she spoke, Margaret Conroy stood up and turned with a smile to the others. 'This is great news—isn't it?' she said, and although her face looked pale, her voice was steady. 'Be sure and congratulate Harold for me—won't you? And now, dears, I must be off, the grand-dad will want his tea, and he mustn't be kept waiting.'

They would have liked to have held her a little longer in conversation, but she seemed in a hurry, and they let her go, watching her wistfully as she moved with her light, graceful steps down the path, and presently they saw her mounting her bicycle at the gate and riding away. 'Well, Annabella, she does not seem as much upset as I had feared,' said Mrs. Hastings.

'I don't know so much about that,' replied her sister. 'I feel sure it was a blow to the girl—and an unexpected one.'

Could they have followed Margaret as she rode home, seen her face, read her thoughts then, they would have known that it had been indeed a blow and a cruel one.

Cross Roads Farm, as her home was called, was but a bare half-mile from Miss Martin's house, and she could have covered the distance in a very short time. But she rode slowly—she could almost have walked as quickly. She wanted to give herself time to think—to ponder over what she had heard.

Margaret Conroy and Harold Hastings had been friends for years—very great friends. And on the part of the girl that friendship had become something deeper. She did not know whether Harold cared for her in that way—perhaps in her inmost heart she guessed that he did not. She had allowed herself to hope that he did—to *think* that he did. Now she had to admit to herself that it had only been a case of 'wishful thinking' on her part. She had put him on a pedestal, worshipped him, and was happy in doing so. It had been enough for her, and she had always had the hope eternal that he would yet give her his love. That had been the way of things up to the present. Never for one moment had Margaret thought that the day might come when he would love another. Yet why she should have been so sure of this she did not know.

'He never gave me any encouragement—never spoke to me as if he cared for me, except as he might have cared for a sister if he had one,' she thought bitterly, as she rode along the familiar road this lovely September day.

'Oh—I was silly—silly! Just a fool of a girl. And it is going to be hard—very hard. How can I hide my real feelings—show a brave face before them all? But I will do it—I will!'

Slowly as she had ridden she was at home now, and saw that old Conroy—the grand-dad as she and Pat called him—was leaning on the gate, watching for her.

'So here ye are at last. A nice time ye've been,' he grumbled, 'leaving me without me tea till this hour.'

'Why, it's barely six, grand-dad.'

'And that's late enough—isn't it? Let ye hurry now and get it ready—because I'm ready for it.'

Margaret went into the house and set about preparing the tea in the big comfortable room leading off the kitchen. Delia Mahony had the kettle boiling for her, and Margaret cut bread and put some eggs on to boil.

Cross Roads Farm was a substantial stone house, and Michael Conroy farmed fifty acres of good land. In spite of his age he was often out and around himself. In fact he was of the opinion that if he did not see to things himself everything would soon go to rack and ruin. Patrick had a hard time of it. He was more up-to-date than the old man and would have wished to run the farm on more modern lines, but this Michael Conroy would not allow. The methods which were the fashion in his youth were still good enough for him, and Patrick's talk could not change him.

'When I'm dead and gone ye can do as ye like—make ducks and drakes of the place, as no doubt ye will. But as long as I'm alive I will be master here.'

Margaret's life was a busy one, between the house, her poultry, the butter-making, and some gardening. She was never idle and had no spare time, in spite of the help given by the stout, middle-aged Delia Mahony, a ready and willing helper, and one who was devoted to Margaret. Delia had been a maid to the girl's mother, and upon her death, when Margaret was but a few years old, had been nurse and friend to the girl ever since.

But busy as she was, Margaret had never found her work hard or uncongenial until this evening—this evening when everything seemed a labour, and she was silent at the tea table where she was generally so full of life and laughter, with gay chatter about her day's doings.

So strange was her silence that the others could not but notice it, and presently Patrick asked: 'Are you not well, Meg?'

'Yes—I am all right. Why do you ask?'

'Well, you haven't said a word since we began tea. What is wrong?'

'Nothing.'

'Well, what's the news from our two old friends over yonder?'

For a moment she hesitated, then she said quietly, and in as indifferent a voice as possible: 'They have great news. Harold has got engaged to a girl in Dublin and he is bringing her down on Saturday to be introduced.'

Patrick stared at her open-mouthed. He was extremely fond of his sister, and her feelings towards Harold were not unknown to him. She had not the slightest idea that he had guessed her secret, but his affection for her had allowed him to read her heart. He gave a soft whistle.

'Well, that is news and no mistake,' he said.

'How do the old people take it?'

'Oh, they seem all right.'

'Pleased?'

'I suppose so—they did not say. Of course they have not met her yet and are very anxious to do so.'

The old man had been listening keenly to all that had been said. His hearing was as good as ever, and he never missed a word that was said. He now looked at Margaret and gave one of his queer chuckles.

'And what do *you* think of it, my dear?' he asked.

The girl flushed painfully in spite of herself. 'It has not much to do with me,' she replied coldly, 'but of course I wish them every happiness.'

'Do you? Do you, indeed?' chuckled the old man. 'Then you are a very good and unselfish girl—very good indeed!'

'I don't know what you mean, grand-dad.'

'Oh, yes you do, my dear. You know quite well. But I am glad you do not intend to wear your heart on your sleeve for the daws to peck at—and that reminds me, Pat, you will need to shoot some of those crows before they do more damage. When I was a young man I would not have needed to be reminded of this kind of work, but I suppose ye have other ways of getting rid of them nowadays—some sort of spraying—something like that. Ah, well, the old ways are good enough for me, so don't let me have to tell you again. I'm off now to take a turn outside with my pipe.'

He left the room, still chuckling to himself as he went. Patrick looked after him in silence for a moment. Then he turned to his sister. He was going to say something to her—what he hardly knew, he felt so terribly sorry for her. But she did not invite his sympathy. Her face was hard and forbidding as she rose to her feet. 'I must help Delia—she is busy this evening,' she said, and so went out, leaving her brother alone.

CHAPTER VII
A BOLT FROM THE BLUE

Nora felt decidedly nervous when the Saturday arrived which was to see her setting off for Wexford in the company of Harold. He could not understand her attitude at all. Why should anyone be nervous meeting his mother and aunt? They were such dears, as he told Nora—no one could help liking them. But how could he know—how could he ever guess—all that the girl had suffered in the past? He knew nothing about that terrible time through which she had gone—that time which had left an indelible impression upon her, so that ever since she was always dreading some revelation about her past. Especially was that so since she had met and loved Harold Hastings. The girl was far from happy. She knew that she should have told him everything before he brought her to his mother as his promised wife. But she had not done so. To herself she acknowledged that she was afraid—abjectly afraid. She simply could not risk losing this man whom she loved so dearly. And so she let the time go by—day after day, week after week—and she had not yet told him. 'I will do so soon—some other time', was the burden of her refrain.

But if anything could have made her forget her worry and anxiety of mind, it would have been the welcome given her by Mrs. Hastings and her sister. No one could have been kinder. They may have felt disappointed that Harold had chosen a girl who was a complete stranger to them, and not one nearer home whom they loved so dearly, and who they knew loved him. But he was free to make his own choice, and they must welcome his future wife, especially when she seemed such a shy little person. So quiet and reserved. So they went out of their way to be nice to her—to let her see that she was really welcome. And after a little while, Nora's shyness and reserve began to melt in the presence of these two old ladies, both of whom were so kind to her. Her visit was going to be a happy one after all. She enjoyed the pleasant tea in the pretty room looking out on the garden where they could see Miss Martin's apple tree standing up proudly, bearing its crop of fruit.

As they chatted gaily, Nora found herself emerging from her shell and telling them about her work at the office, while Harold told of how he and Nora met first on the slopes of Bray Head in the rain. Presently he asked: 'Well, how is everybody here? Old Conroy—I suppose he is still alive?'

'Yes—just the same. A wonderful old man!' replied his mother.

'I don't believe that he will ever die,' said her sister. Then seeing Nora looking at her in some surprise, she explained: 'Michael Conroy is well over ninety. He owns a farm near here, and in spite of his age, is still master there—and very much so! He will not allow Patrick—his great-grandson—to interfere with the working of the place, but insists on having everything his own way—which Patrick says is a hundred years behind the times.'

'And how is Margaret?' asked Harold.

There was an almost imperceptible pause before his aunt replied.

'Margaret is very well,' she said then. 'I asked her to come round this evening, but she had promised to pay a visit to Eileen Madigan—her great friend—you remember her?—who was so ill a short while ago. However, we shall probably see her at Mass tomorrow.'

Nora was wondering who Margaret might be, and Miss Martin, seeing this, thought it best to explain.

'Margaret Conroy is the great-granddaughter of old Michael,' she said, 'she lives with him at Cross Roads Farm and has rather a hard time of it between everything.'

'Oh, Margaret does not mind,' said Harold. 'She is a girl in a thousand—always cheery and gay. I don't believe anything could make her in a bad temper.'

Nora smiled, but said nothing. She suddenly felt decidedly jealous of this other girl whom Harold had known before he had ever met herself. She wondered a little about her before she fell asleep that night. She was occupying the room which was generally kept for Harold, while he was relegated to the sitting-room couch. The cottage had just the two bedrooms with the kitchen and sitting-room, and the sisters slept together, keeping Harold's room always ready for him. But on this occasion it had naturally to be given to Nora.

They discussed the girl for a short time when preparing for bed.

'She seems a nice little thing,' said Mrs. Hastings.

'Yes,' was the reply, 'but rather quiet, and I should say very reserved—able to keep her affairs to herself. I should never have thought that she was the type of girl for whom Harold would have cared—too quiet altogether.'

'I think so, too,' replied Miss Annabella.

A Bolt from the Blue 47

'Margaret seems far more his style. This girl is so shy. I wonder how much he knows about her?'

'Oh, enough, I expect,' said Mrs. Hastings. 'But one never can tell with a young man in love.'

'That's true, Ellen. But still he must surely know something about her family, and so on. No doubt he will tell us soon.'

Miss Martin went to an early Mass at the little church which was but a short distance from the cottage. When she came home to breakfast she told them that she had seen Margaret there, so it was not likely that they would see her at the late Mass in the town, to which they intended going.

'But I was speaking to her,' she added, 'and she said that if possible she would run in to see us before tea. Your bus does not leave too early so you will have time for a chat. She is looking forward to seeing you, too,' she added, turning to Nora with a smile.

So the others went into Wexford and enjoyed the walk there and back, returning with a good appetite for the early dinner, for which Miss Martin had cooked a pair of her own fowl and a fine piece of ham. The meal over, she went into the kitchen to wash up, and put all straight, and Harold, taking off his coat, went with her to help as was his custom when at home, They both refused to allow either Mrs. Hastings or Nora to give any assistance.

'You and mother can sit out in the garden, and get to know one another,' said Harold. And into the garden they went. Mrs. Hastings seated herself in a low chair, while Nora sat at her feet on the grass—just as Margaret had sat a few days ago. It was quite warm for September—being more like a day in August.

Mrs. Hastings was feeling a little curious about this girl to whom her son was evidently so attached. She rather liked her herself, the only thing being that Nora was so reticent, so reserved, saying nothing about her family or her people, seemingly so alone in the world. It was natural, after all, that Harold's mother should wish to know something more about her. So after they talked for a while on indifferent subjects, she said, gently: 'I think Harold told me that both your parents were dead—is that so, my dear?'

'Yes.' Just the bare affirmative—nothing more. But Mrs. Hastings went on: 'You must feel lonely at times. But perhaps you have near relatives?'

'No—I have none.'

'You were an only child then?'

'Yes.'

Mrs. Hastings felt as if there were a stone wall in front of her which she could not pass. How queer it seemed that this girl, who was so soon to be her son's wife—a member of the family—would say nothing about herself or her people. Perhaps if Mrs. Hastings confided in her—told her a little about the troubles of her own life—and Harold's—then maybe Nora, on her part, would give her equal confidence. She might only want a lead—she was so shy.

'Well, I am glad I have my dear sister,' she said. 'I would indeed be lonely without her. She and I have lived together ever since I lost my husband.'

She hesitated a moment, and then asked: 'Has Harold ever told you anything about his father?'

'No, Mrs. Hastings.'

'Well, I expect he would wish you to know about it now that you are about to become his wife. My husband was a fairly wealthy man, but he lost a lot of money—practically his entire fortune—a short time before his death. If this had not happened we should be in a very different position—and Harold quite well off.'

'Oh, I am so sorry,' said Nora, glad that the conversation had now turned on Harold's father and not her own. 'Had he invested it badly?' she asked.

'I have heard Mr. Murphy speak of some worthless shares in which he had lost a lot of money.'

'No—it was not that. It had nothing to do with him personally. The money was stolen from him.'

'Stolen?'

'Yes—stolen. His solicitor, whom he had trusted and treated as a friend, had the money in hand to buy some house property which my husband knew would be a good investment, but instead of using it for that purpose, this man put it to his own use. It appeared that he had been losing a large amount on the Stock Exchange, and so took our money to gamble with—thinking, so people say, that he would be able to retrieve his own fortune and pay back my husband. He lost—not only the little he had left himself, but also every penny belonging to us.'

There was silence for so long that Mrs. Hastings began to wonder if Nora had been listening at all, or had she been simply bored, but then the girl spoke, and if her voice sounded strange in her own ears, the other did not seem to notice it. 'Who was the solicitor—did you ever meet him?' she asked.

A Bolt from the Blue

'No, I never saw him. He and Edward were great friends—but only in a business way. My husband thought the world of him and would have trusted him with untold gold. I know his name, of course.'

'And it was?'

'John Tiernan.'

Again silence—a queer, strained silence. To the girl sitting there, it was as the silence of death—the death of herself and all the world. Her heart seemed to have ceased to beat, the birds no longer sang, coldness and silence was all around. The older woman could not see her face or she might have got a shock, as for the moment it was drained of every particle of colour.

'So you see, my dear,' went on Mrs. Hastings, 'we have had more than our share of trouble—and not through our own fault. That is what Harold says makes it all the harder to bear. But I do not agree with him. I tell him that it is to our credit and we should be glad to know and realise that it was not through his father's carelessness or mistakes that our money was lost—but through the dishonesty of another. I tell him, too, that he ought not to have such bitter feelings towards the memory of John Tiernan, and especially that he should not harbour any thoughts of revenge against his family. The man is dead, he has answered for his own sins. I did not tell you that he took his own life—shot himself. The jury brought in a verdict of temporary insanity—Harold says they always do in such cases, it is more merciful for the survivors. But he insists that John Tiernan was not insane when he took the money—that he was just a thief, and one of the worst kinds of thief, for he took money which was entrusted to him. My poor husband lived but a short time afterwards, he was never strong and the blow killed him. He blamed himself bitterly for not being more careful. As it was, he knew when he was dying that he was leaving us very badly provided for. Harold, who had been brought up to very different prospects, had to turn to and work for us both. He was glad when Mr. Grey offered him a post as clerk in his office. He has been so kind to us, he was a lifelong friend of my dear husband, and helped Harold to become a solicitor and is now going to take him on as partner in the New Year.'

Nora cleared her throat, she knew she would find it difficult to speak, and Mrs. Hastings must not notice her. However, the older woman noticed nothing, she was too full of her subject and went on talking. But Nora could think of but one thing, and when a pause occurred in Mrs. Hastings' speech she asked: 'Is Harold still angry with Mr. Tiernan's family?'

'Yes, indeed he is,' was the reply. 'I never knew him to be so bitter about anything. He does not seem able to forgive the memory of the man who robbed us, or anyone belonging to him who may be alive.'

'And does he know these people?'

'No. We had never met Mrs. Tiernan, but we heard that she died shortly after her husband. There was one daughter, but we have not heard anything of her for some time now. Harold thinks she has probably left the country—perhaps gone to England where she would be unknown. For some time after her father's death we know that she was trying to obtain work as a typist. Harold knew several of the firms to whom she applied, and—against my wishes, for I felt sorry for the poor girl—he advised them not to employ her. He says she is the daughter of a thief and so is not to be trusted. But lately we have heard nothing of her, and I think with Harold that she must be gone away. Now, my dear, this has been a sad tale to tell you, but as you are to be my daughter, we must have no secrets from each other. Now I hope that you have had no trouble of this kind in your life?'

There was a moment's pause. Then Nora sat up looking straight in front of her, her head thrown back, as she replied in clear, cold tones: 'No, indeed, I am glad to say. My father was a commercial traveller. One winter when he was in some wild part of Donegal, he caught a chill and contracted pneumonia. He came home and died a few days later. His death left my mother and myself in poor circumstances; she did not live long after him, and I was lucky enough to get my present job at Murphy's, which I have held ever since.'

Mrs. Hastings gave a little sigh of relief. So after all this girl had nothing of any importance to tell—she was just a shy little thing and had probably felt the death of her parents so deeply that she did not care to talk about her double loss. Had she but known Nora better, her voice and manner would have told her much, but as it was, Mrs. Hastings was quite satisfied with what she had heard.

'Ah, well, my dear,' she said, 'let us hope that the rest of your life may be very happy and so make up for any troubles in the past. And now here are Annabella and Harold. He will have time to take you for a short walk before tea.'

'Come along, Nora,' cried Harold. 'I will show you the Haunted Wood—it's just a bit up the road. Why—what is the matter? You look so pale. Has the mention of the Haunted Wood frightened you?'

'No, indeed. I am not a bit frightened. It would take more than a Haunted Wood to frighten me.'

And Nora sprang to her feet and set off at Harold's side for their walk.

'She is quite all right,' said Mrs. Hastings when the young couple were out of earshot. 'Her father was a commercial traveller, who caught a chill when making his rounds in the country. He contracted pneumonia and did not recover, leaving his wife and daughter very badly off. The wife is dead, but this girl has been working to keep herself.'

'I see. Well, that seems all right.' replied her sister. 'We may have wished him to marry elsewhere, but he is entitled to choose for himself, and like you, I think that Nora Malcolm is a nice little thing—and he might have done much worse.'

CHAPTER VIII

NORA MAKES UP HER MIND

Harold thought that he had never seen Nora in such good spirits as she was during their walk that afternoon. She was talking and laughing, making jokes about everything they saw.

'You are in great spirits,' he said. 'I think that your visit here must have done you good—you are usually such a quiet person.'

'Oh, yes—it has done me a lot of good,' she replied.

'And you like mother and the aunt?'

'Yes, indeed, I think they are delightful. They think a lot of you—don' they?'

'Yes, I am afraid they do—far too much. They have always spoilt me, so you will have to take me in hand and make me find my proper level. Will you be able to do that—do you think?'

'I hope so'—with a gay laugh. 'Oh, I will be a very severe wife— you may be sure of that!' And she laughed again, and Harold laughed with her.

Yet gay as she seemed to be, there was something about Nora which Harold did not understand—a hardness. Even her laughter had lost its sweetness and had the sound of some hard metal—a metallic sound. But still she seemed so gay and bright that he thought he must be fancying all this. 'It is just because she is usually so quiet,' he said to himself, 'she may have been nervous about this visit, and now that it has turned out so well, she is feeling relieved and happy.'

As they went back to the house, Nora observed a tall, dark-haired girl standing at the door. She came forward at once to meet them.

'Hello—Meg!' called out Harold, 'so here you are after all. I was afraid we should have to go without seeing you, and that would never do. Now let me introduce you to the future Mrs. Harold Hastings—you two must be great friends—my all but sister, and my wife to be!'

The two girls looked at each other as they shook hands, and after the way of women, were able to take stock of each other without betraying any especial interest in one another's appearance. Nora saw a pretty girl with soft, dark eyes—dark—blue as she noticed—who said a few words of welcome in low and musical tones. Margaret saw a fair-haired girl, not very tall, with a gay, lively

Nora Makes up Her Mind

manner. Her laugh, indeed, sounded rather loud and Margaret was fairly surprised, as she had received the impression, from what she had been told by the old ladies, that Nora was a quiet, rather shy little person. But this girl was anything but that. She seemed, in fact, to be rather hard, and her laughter had a metallic ring which was unpleasant to the ear. She did not seem at all the kind of girl Margaret had expected to see, and she glanced in wonder at Harold, astonished to observe how much in love he seemed to be.

Tea passed off fairly well. If Mrs. Hastings noticed any change in Nora she attributed it to the fact that the girl was glad the conversation of the afternoon was over. Miss Martin glanced at her curiously now and then, but made no remark. Indeed there was little time to linger over the meal, as Harold and Nora had their bus to catch. So in a short while they had said their goodbyes and were speeding citywards once more.

'Well, dear—what do you think of her?' asked Mrs. Hastings of Margaret.

The girl hesitated. 'She is not quite what I expected,' she replied, 'but that is really your fault. You led me to expect a rather shy person, quiet and reserved. And I should say that Miss Malcolm is not at all that kind of girl.'

'But she is, really,' replied the other. 'Is she not, Annabella?'

'Well, I certainly thought so myself until this evening,' replied her sister. 'But I must say I see a great change in her now.'

'Oh, it is probably because she is glad to have told me all about her father, and how badly she and her poor mother were left.' And she related for Margaret's benefit, the story which Nora had told her.

'Well, yes, of course, she may have felt happier after telling you—but still, I do not think it can explain her very marked change of manner,' replied Miss Martin.

'But she seems a very nice girl, and an extremely pretty one,' said Margaret, 'so let us leave it at that.'

Harold, too, was rather surprised and vaguely puzzled at the change in Nora. All the way homewards in the bus her gay laughter and chatter never ceased, and when he left her at the door of her lodgings the same gay laugh was wafted back at him as he called out, 'goodnight.'

Could he, or any of those who had been with her earlier in the day, have but seen her face as she turned the key in the door and entered the narrow hall, they would have got a shock indeed. They would hardly have known her for the bright girl of a few hours ago. The laughter and gaiety had left that face—wiped out as by one stroke of some unseen hand. Nora was now pale and haggard, her expression was a mask, her every movement automatic. As she was going into her room, the landlady came up the basement stairs.

'Oh, Miss Malcolm, is that you? Such bad news as I'm after having today. Would you believe it—Mrs. Pender is leaving me! She gave me a week's notice this blessed day. What do you think of that?'

Mrs. Pender was the widow of independent means about whom Mrs. Doyle thought so highly—the most select of all her tenants, as she often said. And now she was going to leave. Nora knew what a blow this would be to Mrs. Doyle, and at any other time would have been most sympathetic. But tonight she hardly listened while the woman was speaking—hardly took in the purport of her words. And after a few moments, the landlady noticed this attitude, so unlike Nora's usual manner, and seeing her pale face and haggard expression, suddenly exclaimed: 'But I see you are tired, Miss Malcolm—not feeling ill, I hope?'

'No—I am all right, thank you.'

'All the same, I should not be worrying you with my troubles. I hope you had a nice time today.'

'Yes—very, thank you.'

'Then I will say goodnight, and I hope you will be rested in the morning.'

Mrs. Doyle went away shaking her head and muttering to herself, 'I'm not the only one that has troubles and worries. I never saw Miss Malcolm look so bad—she must be terribly upset about something. I wonder would she have had words with her young man? Well—God help us all—it's a weary world, and that's the truth.'

And she went down to the basement to make herself a cup of strong tea, that being her panacea for all worry.

Left to herself, Nora sat down, and for the first time since she had told her story of falsehoods to Mrs. Hastings, she started to think—to review the situation in her own mind. Well—she had burnt her boats behind her—there was no doubt about that. And she was not sorry. She would do the same thing again. And she

Nora Makes up Her Mind

meant to stick to her story through thick and thin, and risk the danger of the truth coming to light. She could never tell Harold the real facts now—she realised that. And it was rather a relief to her than otherwise. She admitted to herself that she had always dreaded telling him—always put it off from time to time. Now he need never know. Except he heard it from some other source—there was always that danger, she knew that. But if Mary Gilfoyle did not talk about it in the office—and somehow Nora did not think Mary was the sort to do that—then there was little danger. So few people knew that she was the daughter of John Tiernan. How thankful she was now to Michael Derwent for suggesting the change of name . The Derwents knew all, of course, and they might think—indeed they would be sure to do so—that she should have told the truth to Harold. But how could she do so now—now when she knew that he was actually the son of the man whose money her father had wrongfully used? In any case, there was nothing to fear from the Derwents at present. She had received a letter from them a week ago, saying that they had accepted the invitation of a rich American to go with him to New York. They had been delighted to go as it might mean a good deal to Michael. It really seemed, she thought, as if their going just now was quite providential. But she suddenly shuddered at that word. What had she to do with Divine Providence now? Nothing. She was a liar and the daughter of a thief and a suicide. And she was going to marry the man whose father had been robbed by her father. She must be mad! No—she was not mad—only madly in love with Harold. She loved him, and would never give him up if she could manage to keep him. She knew from what Mrs. Hastings had said that he would never marry her—no matter how he loved her—if he knew the facts. Then from her he should never learn them. She would do all in her power to keep him in the dark. All in her power to marry him.

Since that day when she had been to Lilac Tree House, Nora had often wondered if Mrs. Gilfoyle had told her daughters all that she knew about John Tiernan. She had not mentioned anything about him to Nora, but the girl guessed that she knew about the tragedy, and also knew why the girl had changed her name. She had said that the secret was safe with her, but surely she did not mean that she would not tell her girls, although she would probably impose secrecy about the matter. Nora would have liked to have spoken to Mary about it, but could never bring herself to do so. Now, on the morning following her visit to Wexford, she found herself staring earnestly at Mary. But Mary's smile in response, her frank, open countenance, did not seem as if it could hide a secret. Still, Nora would have liked to have spoken to her but could not bring herself to do so. How that day passed she hardly knew, it seemed long and dreary, and she was glad when the hour came for her to go home for her tea. She was just finished when her landlady knocked at her door and entered.

'Good evening, Miss Malcolm,' she said. 'I just looked in to ask how you were? I thought you looked very poorly last night.'

'I am all right, thank you, Mrs. Doyle.'

'Well, I'm glad to hear that, Miss Malcolm. I didn't like the look of you at all last night, and that's a fact. Well, do you remember me telling you that Mrs. Pender was going? It was a real blow to me, for it's not often you get a real lady living on her own means coming to live here—no offence meant, of course, Miss Malcolm. But thanks be to God I have got another lady who will be nearly as good as Mrs. Pender. And strange to say, it was Pat's wife who got me the chance of her. She's the nurse from the Baby Club where she goes with the children—not that I believe much in them places meself—there was none of them in my days, and we managed to look after our babies all right.'

'A nurse—that will be nice for you.'

'Yes—won't it? She's a Miss Mason—a nice, ladylike sort of person, she called round today and saw me. Not too young either, about forty, more or less, I should say. I don't like them as old as that Miss Moran, fussing about that old dog of hers. Her hours, too, will suit me. She is out all day till after five—has her dinner in town, and as you know, Miss Malcolm, the gas cooker is very handy out there on the landing, and like yourself, she can boil her kettle on it at any time.'

'Well, it sounds all right, Mrs. Doyle. When is the lady coming?'

'Mrs. Pender leaves at the end of the week and Miss Mason comes on the following Monday.'

'Well, I hope she will be satisfactory," said Nora, 'and that you get on well together.'

'I hope so, too, Miss Malcolm; but when I think of Mrs. Pender, and all I'm after doing for her, bringing her a cup of tea in her bed when she had a headache, and so on, and then to go and leave me at a moment's notice like this—going to stay with cousins, she says—they're after her bit of money, no doubt—well I just feel that I can trust no one any more. But you will want your tea, and you looking so tired.'

And Mrs. Doyle departed, to Nora's relief.

Nora was not to meet Harold that evening—he was working late with Mr. Grey—but she felt that she could not stay in her room by herself—thinking—thinking. So she went for a walk. She was physically tired after her day in the office and restless night, but she could not stay still. She felt she could not even sit quiet in the tram—she must keep moving. So she walked to the Dartry terminus and then turned up the Dodder, coming home again by Terenure and Rathgar. It was a beautiful evening and a beautiful walk, but Nora was blind to the loveliness around her; she could think of nothing but her trouble, she could not keep her thoughts from dwelling upon her terrible problem. She might just as well have stayed at home, except that she hoped the walk might tire her and so make her sleep. But it did not do so. There are times when the mental condition of a person is more powerful than the physical. Nora went to bed early, trying—hoping—to fall asleep soon. But all was useless, her body was indeed tired, but her mind was active. Over and over again she went through all that Mrs. Hastings had said to her—her every word was written on her brain in burning characters—never to be forgotten. And she remembered all that she had told Mrs. Hastings. Lies—lies. That was what she had told to Harold's mother. If only it had been lies that the other had told her. But she knew this was not so.

The summer dawn had long appeared in the sky before at last Nora fell into a troubled sleep, to dream of dreadful things—and to awaken to a dreadful reality.

CHAPTER IX

ROSE HEARS SOME NEWS

The days went by somehow for Nora. She met Harold nearly every evening, and with him was always bright and apparently happy. At times he was faintly puzzled by her manner, but did not think much about it. All girls have moods, he told himself—or so he had heard. Margaret, of course, was different, she was always serene and happy. So patient, too, with that old Michael Conroy, so crossgrained and hard to manage. But all the same, Margaret was not the girl he loved. Harold had guessed long ago that his mother and aunt would have wished him to marry Margaret Conroy, and it might have been that if he had not met Nora he would have done so. But he *had* met her. Met her and loved her, almost at first sight. And now that he knew what love really was, he knew also that Nora was the one woman in the world for him. Margaret was like a sister to him, a dear sister of whom he would always be very fond, but marry her? Never.

He often spoke of their own marriage to Nora. Like all young couples, they would talk about the future and plan what they would do. They were undecided as to whether they should start life in a flat or take a small house in the suburbs. They discussed the pros and cons of each idea, Harold being inclined for the flat.

'We could move into a house later—a nice house, too, better than we can afford at present,' he said.

'I just want to feel my way and see how the firm of Grey and Hastings will prosper.'

Nora, on the other hand, favoured a small house which she could run herself with just a woman in to help once a week. They studied the advertisements in the papers, both of houses and flats, and sometimes went to see some of them. But there never seemed to be anything just suitable, and as the wedding was not to be till January they both felt that there was no need to hurry.

In October, Mary Gilfoyle had influenza rather badly and was absent for some weeks from the office. A temporary typist was engaged in her place with whom Rose Malone made friends at once, the newcomer seeming quite fascinated with her. They were very intimate before a week had passed and used to go out to lunch together. All the girls in the office, and a good many of those

Rose Hears Some News

engaged in the sales department, were in the habit of frequenting a nearby restaurant for their mid-day meal. It was convenient to their work, and they had been going there for so long now, that they were well known and the waitresses would keep their seats for them in the rush hour.

Nora was sitting at her usual table one day at which there happened to be a vacant chair. She had ordered her lunch, and was looking round when she saw Rose and the new typist seated at a table nearby. Rose did not always come here, and Nora nodded coldly in response to her wave of the hand. She then turned her attention to the magazine she had brought with her.

Suddenly she heard a voice at her elbow exclaiming: 'Why—Nora Tiernan! Who would have thought of meeting you here! It is ages since we met! But you know I have been in England for over two years.'

The speaker was a stout, voluble lady of middle age, rather showily dressed. Nora recognised her as a woman who had been their near neighbour in Rathgar in the happy days which now seemed so long ago. She and her husband had gone to England—where he had obtained some business appointment—just about the time John Tiernan's tragedy had taken place.

Nora was struck literally speechless at this encounter. That one should have come across this woman whom she had believed to be in England—and here in this restaurant, with Rose Malone sitting within earshot of all that passed—it was a blow indeed.

But the lady was talking away: 'Well, how are you, my dear? I cannot say that you look well. But no wonder—you must still suffer from what you went through that dreadful time. And your poor mother has passed away too? Ah—it was all too terrible. But tell me now, how are you getting on? What are you doing?'

But Nora could stand no more. Rose's face, as she sat there, seemingly drinking in every word that Mrs. Farrell uttered, was too much for her to bear. She rose to her feet even while the waitress was placing her meal before her.

'Excuse me,' she murmured, 'I—I am not well.'

'Oh, I am so sorry,' exclaimed Mrs. Farrell. 'Let me come with you—call a taxi—you are not fit to be alone.'

But Nora, with a hasty gesture, gathered up her purse, bag, and gloves and hurriedly left—flying she hardly knew whither—feeling as if the foul fiend himself were in pursuit.

The lady whom she had left in such an unceremonious fashion stared after her in amazement. What could be the matter? She remembered Nora Tiernan as a quiet, shy little thing, and she must have felt her father's disgrace acutely. Still, it had all happened three years ago, and she had surely had time to get over it—at least to some degree. Was she really ill? Or was there something else the matter? While she was thus thinking she felt a touch on her arm. Turning round, she saw Rose Malone, who said, in her most engaging manner: 'You will pardon me, I am sure, but I was wondering if Miss Malcolm was not well—she left so hurriedly?'

'Miss Malcolm?' echoed Mrs. Farrell. 'I do not know anyone of that name.'

'I mean the young lady you were just speaking to.'

'That is Miss Tiernan,' was the reply.

'Miss Tiernan? How strange! She is in the same office as myself, and we have always known her as Miss Malcolm—is that not so, Miss McGrane?'

The other girl nodded in assent, her eyes and ears open in surprise. As Mrs. Farrell stared at Rose in puzzled silence, that young lady said: 'Perhaps I should not have said so much—but of course I did not know that you knew her under another name.'

Now Mrs. Farrell was an exceedingly talkative woman, there was nothing she liked so much as a gossip, also her curiosity was aroused about Nora Tiernan. So she smiled graciously at Rose.

'Not at all,' she replied. 'Have you lunched? No? Then let us share a table, shall we?'

And so when Rose Malone left the restaurant she was in full possession of Nora's real name, and of all the facts relating to her father's disgrace and suicide.

To the surprise of the girl with her, Rose enjoined strict secrecy as they went back to the office.

'We do not want to get the poor thing into trouble,' she said, 'so why should we tell what we know—talk about it to others? As long as she keeps honest and is earning her livelihood it would be cruel to broadcast her story. So now not a word of what we have heard— I depend upon you to keep a silent tongue in your head abut the matter.'

Miss McGrane was disappointed. She had looked forward to the bombshell which would be thrown into the office when this extraordinary tale was unfolded—had felt quite a thrill of rather pleasureable excitement. She was puzzled too. She had not given Rose credit for showing so much consideration towards another girl—especially one whom she had never liked. But evidently she had misjudged her. She had to promise to say nothing, and, in any case, she would be leaving soon when Miss Gilfoyle returned.

Rose was very quiet all that afternoon. She took little notice of Nora, sitting, whitefaced and wretched, but if their eyes chanced to meet, would smile in a friendly way, so that Nora began to think that perhaps Rose had not heard what Mrs. Farrell had been saying. She hoped not with all her might, for once Rose knew of it she was sure that the story would be broadcast everywhere. But the days passed—a fortnight—and then Mary Gilfoyle returned to work and Miss McGrane left.

'Now remember,' said Rose to her, 'you are to keep a still tongue in your head about Miss Malcolm if you want to keep friends with me and to come to that dance I promised you. Can I depend on you?'

'Oh, of course, Miss Malone. I should not dream of going against your wishes in this matter.'

'Very well, then—don't forget. And perhaps I may be able to do you a good turn before long.'

And all this time Nora was in torment of mind. Now that she looked back upon her meeting with Mrs. Farrell she saw that she had acted in a stupid manner. She should have greeted Mrs. Farrell quietly, asked her to call at her lodgings, told her everything—all she had gone through, and that it had been upon the advice of Michael Derwent that she had changed her name, and that only then had she obtained work. Mrs. Farrell was not an unkind woman and would certainly have kept her secret, but she, herself, had spoilt everything by running away like that. What could the woman think? Now she might talk, and being such a gossip she was almost sure to do so, and then everything would come to light. All Nora's deception—her lies—all would have been in vain. Was there nothing that she could do? She could think of nothing. Then, as the days passed and she heard no more about the matter, Nora began to hope again—to believe, or make believe—that Mrs. Farrell had returned to England, and nothing further would be heard from her. Had Rose given the slightest sign that she knew anything she would not have been so easy in mind, but Rose was seemingly so innocent of the whole thing that it was almost certain she had learnt nothing. Nora could not think that Rose would be able to keep such news to herself. No—it seemed that after all she must not have heard Mrs. Farrell words.

Nora began to breathe once again. Once more she put far from her the memory of her father's disgrace. Ever since she had told her untrue story to Mrs. Hastings she had tried to imagine that she was really the daughter of that poor commercial traveller who had caught a chill while going his rounds in Donegal and died from pneumonia. She tried never to think of the real facts.

Yet happy she could not be at this time. Nora had never been very religious, her spiritual nature was not yet awakened. She had gone to Mass on Sundays and Holydays of Obligation and had approached the Sacraments once a month. But lately she had not been to Confession for some time. How could she go? she asked herself. She might try and imagine in her own mind that she was not the daughter of a thief, but in her heart she knew the truth; knew, too, that she would have to confess her deception before she could receive Holy Communion. So Nora kept away from the Sacraments, and tried to forget that she had once been a better Catholic.

CHAPTER X
'WHAT IS YOUR NAME?'

'Well, I know I left it there—in the drawer of my table. I remember putting it there!'

'What have you lost, Mary?' asked Nora, who had just come back from lunch.

'My fountain pen—I cannot find it anywhere—yet I know I left it there.'

'When did you put it in the drawer?' asked Rose Malone.

'Just before I went out to lunch. I always put it in the same place—the little drawer of my table.'

'And you cannot find it?'

'No. I have searched everywhere, but it seems to have vanished.'

'Oh, it will be sure to come to light again,' said Nora.

'I hope it won't be like the gloves I lost last week,' said Rose, I have never found them—and they were a good pair, too.'

'Or like my blue scarf,' chimed in Kitty Dunne,

'I never found that, and it's a week now since it disappeared.'

'Well, I would not have lost my pen for anything,' said Mary, 'mother gave it to me last Christmas, and I will miss it terribly.'

This was the beginning of a series of petty thefts from the office. No one could understand it, and a feeling of constraint and tension was all around. Rose kept lamenting her gloves. Mary—although not so constantly—her fountain pen. Then came the day when Kitty Dunne found that her purse had been taken from her handbag as it hung on the wall with her coat in the little recess where the girls kept their outdoor things.

The only one who had lost nothing was Nora. She remarked upon this one day when they were discussing the matter. 'I seem to be the lucky one,' she said. 'It is strange that I have lost nothing.'

'Yes—*very* strange,' replied Rose. There was a moment's silence, while no one spoke, each of the girls feeling suddenly uncomfortable. They had never felt like this before, but there had been such a queer intonation in Nora's voice as she made the seemingly innocent remark that they found themselves looking at Nora almost as if she had been a stranger in their midst. For her part, Nora did not at first attribute any particular meaning to Rose's words, and it was not for a moment or two that she sensed the atmosphere of the room, the queer looks of the others. She flushed vividly and turned to her work. No one said anything further then, but when the hour came to leave the office that evening, Rose rather ostentatiously walked out with Kitty Dunne, taking no notice of Nora. But Mary Gilfoyle stayed behind, saying with a laugh: 'Rose seems to have got a bee in her bonnet about all these petty thefts. But what can we do? I cannot think who can have done it. What is your opinion, Nora?'

She was surprised to see how uncomfortable and ill at ease Nora seemed to be, as she replied shortly:'I have no opinion about it at all.'

'But who could have stolen the things?' asked Mary. 'There is nobody in the office besides ourselves. Mrs. Grace—the cleaner—is gone before we come in the morning. No one could go near our things without us seeing them. Who can have taken them?'

'I have said that I do not know—why keep on asking me?'

Nora coloured angrily as she spoke and Mary looked at her in astonishment. She was perfectly well aware that Rose, from pure spite and badness of heart, was trying to throw the blame on Nora, and Mary was only anxious to get Nora to say something—make some remark—which would show her innocence. Not that Mary doubted her for a moment—she was much more inclined to suspect the fair Rose. But how queer Nora was in her manner. Mary could not make her out at all, and when she tried to speak on the matter again, Nora said that she was sick of the whole subject, and turned the conversation. Mary could not but feel puzzled and annoyed. That Nora was guilty had not as yet crossed her mind for an instant but now the girl's strange attitude could not but sow some seeds of doubt in her mind, and she said good-night rather coldly when their ways parted.

Nora made her way home to Rathmines, perturbed and wretched. Who did it—what could it all mean? Why had Rose made that remark and then looked at her in such a manner that the other girls became suspicious too? Did Rose really believe that she— Nora—had taken the things? As if she would do such a thing! 'But you are the daughter of a thief—perhaps you are following in your father's footsteps.' That was what people might say of her. But before anyone could think like that they must know about her father, and Rose did not. But was this certain? Nora suddenly remembered the day when Mrs. Farrell had been in the restaurant and had remained behind with Rose. Could she have spoken to her? Told her everything? But no—she would not believe that. Besides, if she had done so, Rose would have at once talked about it to the whole office. Disliking Nora as she did, it was not likely that she would have let such an opportunity pass.

It was a quiet Nora who set out to meet Harold that evening. They were going to the Gaiety to see *The Student Prince*, and at any other time Nora would have enjoyed herself greatly, for this was one of her favourite musical plays. But tonight, her torment of mind was so great that she could hardly follow the play—it seemed a meaningless jumble to her and she wished it were over so that she could go home and think things out in quietness.

Harold could not fail to notice her lack of interest.

'Are you not well, darling?' he asked in the interval. 'Would you like some tea or coffee?'

'No, thank you, Harold. I am all right—just a bit of a headache.'

'Then a cup of tea will help you—let us go into the cafe.'

But she would not. She shrank from meeting anyone, only desired to be back in her own room and try to think things out. But when later she found herself there, her mind was in such a state that she found it well-nigh impossible to concentrate on what was best to be done—what steps to take. If she could only have seen Mrs. Farrell, had a talk with her, begged her to keep her secret. But she did not even know her address, foolishly she had not waited to ask for it—had only thought of running away as soon as possible from one who knew of her past. Had Rose Malone not been there, sitting so close, listening—or seeming to do so—Nora might not have fled so hastily, thus annoying Mrs. Farrell who thought her very rude. No—there was nothing she could do now. Only wait and hope for the best, while fearing the worst.

She had not long to wait—and it was the worst which came to her.

Rose Malone thought that the time had now come to take action—strike against this girl whom she hated with an unreasoning hatred. So a few mornings later she knocked at the door of Mr. Murphy's private room.

'Come in!'

Mr. Michael Murphy, head of the firm of Murphy and Co. glanced up in some surprise as she entered. It was not usual for the office staff to come to his room unsummoned.

'Good morning, Miss Malone,' he said. 'Did you want to see me?'

Rose acted her part well—she was, indeed, what is known as a born actress. Lifting her eyes timidly, she faltered, 'Yes, please, Mr. Murphy.'

'Well—what is it? You know I am rather busy at this hour.'

'I—I am afraid that you will not be very pleased at what I have to say—in fact that you may be very upset. But I felt it my duty to let you know about it.'

'Well, well—what is it?'

Michael Murphy was rather an impatient man at times, and he hated above all else to be disturbed when he was just sitting down to open his morning correspondence. He felt inclined to tell this girl to come back another time when he had more leisure—Mr. Cannon would be in at any moment to take his orders—but he thought it best to let her have her say and be finished with the matter. As she still hesitated, he said curtly: 'You must be quick with whatever you have to say—as I told you, I am busy just now.'

So she told him then about the things which had been stolen lately from the office—one thing after another. Mary's pen, her own gloves—'But when Miss Dunne's purse was taken, I thought it best to let you know,' she said.

Mr. Murphy was annoyed. Such a thing had not happened before in the office. He questioned Rose as to whether any stranger—any chance caller—could have been the culprit. but she explained that the office was never left alone, one girl taking it in turn to remain during the lunch hour, to deal with callers or telephone messages. The office was quite apart from the sales department.

He asked then about the office cleaner. 'Mrs. Grace is always gone before we arrive,' replied Rose.

'Who was left in the office during lunch hour on the day Miss Dunne missed her purse?' he asked.

Rose seemed to hesitate—to dislike answering. Then in low voice, she said, 'Miss Malcolm.'

Something in her manner caused Mr. Murphy to glance sharply at her.

'Miss Malcolm?' he repeated.

'Surely you do not suspect *her* of all people?'

Rose was furious when she heard the note of incredulity in his voice. So he considered Nora to be above suspicion, did he? She would open his eyes. And suddenly—before she had meant to do

'What is Your Name?'

so—she had said: 'Do you know Miss Malcolm's real name? Who she really is?'

Mr. Murphy stared at her. 'What do you mean, Miss Malone?'

'Just what I say, Mr. Murphy. Will you ask Miss Malcolm—as she calls herself—her real name, and if she tells you the truth I think you will get rather a surprise.'

Michael Murphy did not speak for a moment. An astute man, he was quick to see that this girl hated Nora for some reason, and that she wished to do her harm was plain to be seen. Well, he would give her no satisfaction, but he would certainly enquire into the matter himself.

'That will do, Miss Malone,' he said. 'Thank you for letting me know about the trouble in the office. You may go now.'

Rose hesitated for a moment, she would have dearly liked to say more, but one glance at her employer's face told her that there was no more to be said, and she left the room, wondering if she had been wise to tell him at all. Yet she had planned everything so well, she had been so sure of being able to revenge herself upon Nora for all that girl's aloofness and pride. But Mr. Murphy seemed to think that Nora was above suspicion, and this attitude on his part had caused Rose to lose her temper, so that she had spoken too hastily, undoing everything. Yet surely she had made him suspicious? He could not let her words pass quite unnoticed.

He could not. Left to himself, Michael Murphy went over her words again. What in the world could the girl have meant when she told him to ask Miss Malcolm to give her real name? Her real name? Such a nice little thing, Nora Malcolm—he had always liked her—that is, what he had seen of her, for he left the control of the office staff mostly in the hands of Mr. Cannon, his business manager. He rang for him now.

'Cannon,' he said, when the manager entered, 'what do you think of that little typist—Miss Malcolm?'

Mr. Cannon slightly raised his eyes. It was seldom that Mr. Murphy troubled himself about any of the staff.

'Miss Malcolm?' he repeated, 'she is all right, sir—a capable, good worker.'

'You are sure her name is Malcolm?'

'Sure her name is Malcolm!' Mr. Cannon stared at Mr. Murphy in bewilderment. Really only that he knew Mr. Murphy was a Pioneer——

'Why, of course, sir,' he replied, 'Nora Malcolm is her name.'

Then Mr. Murphy told him all that Rose had said. Mr. Cannon listened quietly, then shrugged his shoulders.

'I should not take much notice of what Miss Malone says,' he replied. 'She is not always to be relied upon.'

'Still I think we should get to the bottom of this—all those petty thefts, and so on, are very annoying. Don't you agree, Cannon?'

'Certainly, sir, if you think it worth while.'

'Then ring, will you, and ask Miss Malcolm to come here.'

Mr. Cannon did so, and a moment later Nora entered. She was pale and nervous, being perfectly sure that a call to go to Mr. Murphy could only mean something unpleasant for her now. Were not the fates against her? And was she not being caught in a trap from which there was no escape?

'Miss Malcolm,' said Mr. Murphy, quietly, 'I have requested you to come here in order to ask you just one question—to which I shall expect a complete and truthful reply.'

'Yes, Mr. Murphy.'

She knew her voice was trembling, in spite of all her efforts to keep it under control.

'Then will you kindly tell me your name?'

So it had come—the hour which she had always dreaded. She could not speak, her lips were too dry. She could only stand there in frozen silence. Mr. Murphy waited a moment, then asked again—at the same time feeling a strange reluctance—as if he were torturing some dumb creature—to probe further.

'Your name, please.'

Then she spoke. Of what avail was it to keep the knowledge from him? He would know sooner or later. Rose must have heard all and told it to him. He had only to go to Mrs. Farrell and enquire for himself.

She moistened her lips and spoke.

'My name is Nora Tiernan,' she said, and lifted her head proudly, glad that she could once again own to the name of which she had been so proud in the old days. Then, as Mr. Murphy did not speak, she went on: 'I am the daughter of John Tiernan, who took money belonging to one of his clients, gambled and lost all and then shot himself. You will remember the case?'

Mr. Murphy and his manager stared at her. They hardly knew this pale-faced girl, who stood there so proudly. She might have been announcing that she was a king's daughter, so bravely and scornfully did she face them. Neither of them spoke, and Nora said quietly: 'You think that because I am my father's daughter I took the things which are missing from the office. I know you think so. But I did not—I never touched them. I know nothing about them.'

Mr. Murphy did not know what to do—what to think. He glanced at the manager, and saw that he, too, was puzzled. But one thing was clear—the girl could not be kept any longer in his employment. He was sorry for her, standing there, with her tragic eyes, but then he knew little of her and could not tell whether she were innocent or not as regards the office thefts. But she was her father's daughter. Rose Malone knew this and would tell the others. Even if he kept on Nora Malcolm—or rather Nora Tiernan—she would be sure to have a bad time, the other girls would not be friendly, they would always believe that she had taken the things. And perhaps she had. How was he to know? It looked very fishy, to say the least of it, and Michael Murphy hated deceit of any kind. The girl had been living under an assumed name. She had no right to do so—she must go. It would be the best step to take in the interest of everyone. He cleared his throat, preparatory to giving her notice—for somehow he did not like to do so. But Nora did not wait for him to speak.

'I see that you wish me to leave, Mr. Murphy,' she said, 'and I am ready to do so at once.'

'Well, I am afraid that I must ask you to go,' replied Mr. Murphy. 'I am sorry, as you have always given satisfaction; but now with this trouble in the office, and the rest of the staff knowing about your name, and so on—Mr. Cannon will give you a cheque for a month's salary in lieu of notice, and with regard to references, I will give you a good one as regards your work.'

'But not as regards my honesty—I understand,' replied the girl, 'but I will not trouble you for either your reference or your cheque.' And turning on her heel Nora left Mr. Murphy's office.

The two men stared at one another in perplexity.

'I wonder have I done right?' murmured Mr. Murphy. 'If that girl should be honest after all.'

'If I may say so, sir, you took the only possible course in the circumstances. You could not have kept the girl in the face of what we know. This sort of affair only convinces me more strongly than ever that it is a mistake to employ women in business. They were never meant for it, and are not fit for it in any way.'

'There I disagree with you,' said Mr. Murphy. 'They are fitted for many positions in the business world, and they certainly make the best typists and very good secretaries, too. And they are conscientious and hard-working—much more than men.'

'And jealous and sentimental, too. This affair gives us a good example of it.'

'But think of how cheap they are in comparison with men. I could not offer a man the salary I give to one of those girls.'

'That is true,' agreed Mr. Cannon. 'And now, sir, what about that letter to Messrs. Doyle and Co?'

CHAPTER XI

TERESA MASON

Teresa Mason had just come home to her tea. She was a woman in the early forties, of medium build, with dark-grey eyes and clear-cut features. Tired after her day's work in the district, going up and down stairs of the tenements, she filled her kettle from the tap on the landing and put it on the gas to boil. The room in which she presently sat down to take her tea looked pretty and cosy this chilly evening in late October. Teresa had put a match to the fire and the firelight shone on her books and pictures. Mrs. Doyle had let the room 'partly furnished,' but Teresa had some good bits of furniture of her own, and altogether this bed-sittingroom was home-like and pleasant and a place to which Teresa was always glad to return after her day's work.

While she was enjoying her tea, there was a knock at the door and Mrs. Doyle entered. She carried a bowl in her hand.

'I am sorry to trouble you, Miss Mason,' she said, 'but could you possibly oblige me with a little bit of sugar? There's George come in for his tea earlier than usual, and didn't I forget the sugar when I was up Rathmines today. And he's such a terrible one for sugar in his tea.'

'Why—of course, Mrs. Doyle,' and Teresa filled the bowl.

'I don't know whether you have seen Miss Malcolm?' said the landlady then.

'No—I have not. Perhaps she is not yet back from the office:'

'Oh, yes, she is,' was the reply, 'she came back early this morning and has not been out since.'

'Is she not well?'

'That's more than I can tell you. I knocked at her door about dinner time to ask if I could do anything for her, but she just said no—she only wanted to be left alone—quite huffy she seemed!'

'Oh, she must be feeling ill,' said Teresa, 'otherwise she would surely never have come home so early.'

'I was wondering whether you would have a look at her—being a nurse and all—just to see if you think she's all right? She is a real nice little thing and I feel a bit worried about her, and that's a fact.'

'But she might not like me to interfere.'

'Oh, she won't mind you, I'm sure. You could make the excuse to ask her for a match, or something like that.'

'All right,' agreed Teresa, 'I will try after I have finished my tea.' And Mrs. Doyle withdrew, looking relieved.

A little later Teresa knocked at the door across the landing. For a moment there was no reply, then in low tones a voice said, 'Come in.' Teresa entered, and Nora, thinking it was the landlady, did not look round, but only asked, 'Well, Mrs. Doyle—what is it?'

Teresa saw that Nora was sitting huddled in a chair, and there was neither fire nor light in the room—and only illumination coming from the street lamp which stood close to the front gate. There was something about her attitude—about the whole atmosphere of the room—so cold and comfortless, that Teresa felt a real pang of pity for this girl whom she knew so slightly. 'It is not Mrs. Doyle,' she said gently. 'I hope you will forgive me for troubling you, but could you oblige me with a match?'

She felt foolish while she made the request, she had plenty of matches—surely this quiet girl would easily see through such a flimsy excuse. But Nora seemed—and was—absolutely indifferent—as she turned round and saw Teresa standing just inside the door. 'There is a box there on the table—take what you want,' she replied shortly.

'I am afraid I shall have to switch on the light—I cannot see very well,' said Teresa.

'No—please don't—here are the matches,' and Nora, rising from her seat, found the matches and handed them to Teresa.

Her voice sounded so tired and weary that Teresa took courage and asked: 'Won't you let me put a match to your fire—I see it is ready set—and the evening is getting very cold.'

'No, thank you. I do not need it,' was the reply.

Teresa hesitated, standing there on the threshold. She knew that there was something wrong here, this girl was either ill or in some trouble, and somehow Teresa felt almost sure that it was trouble of mind and not illness of body. But it would be best to pretend otherwise.

'Miss Malcolm,' she said, 'are you not well? Forgive me for asking—but you do not seem to be well. Please do let me light the fire and get you some hot tea—I can boil the kettle in my room in a minute—you will feel better after it.'

'I want nothing, thank you. And if I did I could get it for myself. I only wish to be left alone—in peace.'

After that there was no more to be said, and Teresa, taking a couple of matches from the box for the sake of appearances, left the room. She felt sorry for the girl, but after all, she knew her very slightly, and it was obvious that she did not wish for any sympathy in her trouble—whatever it was. Still several times that evening, as she sat before the cheerful fire in her pleasant room, Teresa found herself thinking of that lonely little figure across the landing. She would have been only too glad to help or advise in any way had the other seemed to want it, but far from wanting it, Nora had definitely repulsed any overtures in that direction.

'I wonder what is the matter?' thought Teresa,

'I suppose it is the usual tiff with her "boy friend". Oh—these foolish young people!'

And Teresa smiled and sighed, remembering one who had given his life for Ireland in 1916 and whose earthly remains now lay in a patriot's grave, while his soul walked with the Blest in Heaven above. As she sat there by her fire on that evening in 1936—twenty years afterwards—she could see again the gallant boy marching forth on that April morning. Well, he had done all he could, had gladly given his life for his country.

Teresa, looking back now, saw again through a mist of tears the one who had been so dear to her—and yet whom she had not grudged to Dark Rosaleen.

How handsome he had been—how brave, and how much she, then a girl in her early twenties, had loved him—loved him so that she could never afterwards think of another man as a lover. Yet Desmond Pierce was remembered by few now. His parents were dead and he had been an only child. There was but one person with whom Teresa could talk about her dead hero, and that was an old, old man down in County Wexford. He and Desmond had been near neighbours, and old Michael Conroy loved to talk about the gallant boy who had been one after his own heart. An aunt of Teresa had lived in the same place for many years, and Teresa as a schoolgirl, and afterwards as a 'pro' in training, used to spend her holidays there. That was how she had met Desmond; and although that was many a year ago and Desmond was gone, and her aunt, too, Teresa even now often spent a week or so of her holidays with the Conroys. She liked Margaret and her brother, but above all she loved the old man. Perhaps there were not many who loved Michael Conroy—with the exception of Greyleg, his pony, and Judy, his little black cocker—but among those few must be counted Teresa Mason. He could talk to her of those who were gone; could tell her of the Fenian Rising of '67, could remember as if yesterday the glorious days of 1916. Margaret and Pat had been but tiny children then, too young to recall anything of that time. But Michael Conroy remembered it all.

And Teresa was going there again soon now—next week, in fact. She was thinking with pleasure about that this very evening. There was a week's holiday due to her, she had been working very hard of late and the doctor had advised a rest. So in four days' time she was off to the country—to the Conroy's farm, outside Wexford town.

And little did she imagine that Margaret Conroy's love dream had been shattered by the lonely girl in the room across the landing.

Teresa saw but little of Nora during the few days before she set off for Wexford. Mrs. Doyle had told her that Miss Malcolm was not returning to her employment. 'I think she had been dismissed,' said the landlady, 'and she is feeling it too—very badly. Well, I hope she soon gets another job—both for her sake and my own. Not that she owes me any rent at present, but no work—no rent. That's what I always found with my tenants.'

'Is she well, do you think?' asked Teresa.

'Well, enough, although a bit washed-out—off her food, I expect with the worry. As I often say to Pat's wife—"If you have your friend in your pocket, you are all right—and the whole world is your friend—but it is the other way round if you've no money."'

'Does Miss Malcolm go out much?'

'Yes—she's out pretty near all day—looking for a job, I suppose. She used to have a young man—a nice fellow, too—calling for her, taking her to the theatre and seeing her home, and so on, but I never see him now, and she doesn't go out at night at all. I'm afraid he has jilted her—so I am.'

'I am sorry to hear that,' replied Teresa. 'Be as kind to her as you can, Mrs. Doyle. Poor thing—she must be going through a bad time just now.'

But Nora did not want anyone to give her sympathy or to talk to her. She went her own way, speaking only when it was absolutely necessary to do so. It so happened that Harold was away for a fortnight, having gone to Belfast on some legal business, and Nora was trying to get another job before he returned. She wanted to be able to say that she left Mr. Murphy of her own accord and had obtained a better post. Her future relations with Harold she left to Fate. But she was determined that as long as he learnt nothing from others he would certainly learn nothing from her. She would never tell him. Fate might do its worst and it surely seemed to be against her, but she would never give in—she would fight, would blazon it out, until the end. In the meantime she might get work—that was the most important matter of all at the moment. Feverishly she tried to get some position. She replied to every advertisement which might be suitable, walking from place to place, hoping against hope. But she was always met with the same question—Where had she been employed, and where was her reference? She could not give any satisfactory answers, and so was passed over. She tried to buoy herself up with hope, but it was hard work. Dreary, hopeless and desolate seemed her life at that moment. And over all hung the fear that, by some unforeseen happening, Harold might discover her secret. What would then be his reaction?

* * * *

It was a lovely day in October when Teresa Mason arrived at the Conroys' farm. Margaret met her at the bus stop, and old Michael was waiting for her at the gate. She ran forward and took his wrinkled old hand in both her strong ones. 'Oh, Mr. Conroy, I'm so glad to see you again!' she cried.

'And amn't I glad to see yourself!' was the reply.

Teresa was one of the very few towards whom old Michael showed any affection; even with his great-grandchildren he was cross and difficult—as they knew too well. But he felt differently with Teresa. She could remember clearly those days in 1916—days which the younger generation seemed either unable or unwilling to remember. The old man had no use for these modern youngsters growing up all around him.

'It seems all they think about is going to the pictures or dances. Dances—save the mark! If they *were* dances, who would object? But they just walk up and down, twisting their bodies about, and they call it dancing. And the music! The gulls that do be screaming when they're looking for food are more like music than the noise made by so-called dance bands today. Such screeching and yelling I never heard. In my day both dancers and noisemakers would have been turned out of any dance. But then we knew *how* to dance.'

He lamented thus as usual to Teresa as they sat by the big turf fire after a substantial tea. Teresa sat on a low stool beside him, and Margaret was opposite. Old Conroy drew slowly at his pipe as he went over the events, the customs and manners of his youth.

'Why, I declare to God,' he said, 'when I look around today and see the way the people do be going on, I often ask meself is it a heathen country I'm in and not Ireland at all? And to think that it was for this sort of thing that our best men laid down their lives!'

'But, Mr. Conroy, all the young people are not spending their time at the pictures or jazz dances,' said Teresa. 'In Dublin there are hundreds of really Irish boys and girls learning the language, holding their own dances, acting Irish plays.'

'Mebbe so—mebbe so, but down here they seem to have gone quite mad.'

'Oh, no—not all, grandfather,' interposed Margaret, 'your know there are many just like those Teresa spoke about. Look at the Kavanaghs and the Dalys——'

'Yes—and look at me own great-grandson going off to the pictures two or three times a week when he might be doing something useful here.'

'Oh, well, Mr. Conroy,' said Teresa, 'young people must have some amusement, you know, all work and no play doesn't do.'

'There's a right and a wrong way to amuse themselves. And listen to them talking! I heard young Sean McGrath calling to Mary Cullen the other evening, "OK Baby—I'll be seeing you!" and that was meant for goodnight, if you please—what do you think of that? Oh, for the days when an Irish salutation was heard on the lips of our people, and not echoes of that Hollywood place.'

'Poor grandfather—he cannot move with the times at all,' said Margaret, when she and Teresa were getting ready for bed that night. The old man had given out the Rosary at the stroke of ten, and now the two girls were in Margaret's bedroom, which Teresa always shared when at the farm. She said now, in reply to Margaret's remark, 'Well, I don't think that I should care to see him other than he is. He is such a dear old man,' she added with a smile. Then she said, 'Now tell me, is there any news since I was here last? Your letters have not been very full of news, you know.'

As she spoke, she saw a shadow pass over her friend's face, and she glanced curiously at her. She had noticed at once that Margaret had changed in some queer way. All the brightness and happiness had gone from her face. She was quieter, too, much quieter. She had tried to hide the change and wondered at it. What had happened to her friend? Neither the old man nor Pat seemed to see any difference in her, but perhaps they were used to it by now. But Teresa saw it, and when Margaret did not speak for the moment, she asked quietly: 'What is it, dear? Something has happened since last we met—won't you tell me?'

But Margaret could not do so. How could she? She had told no one, spoken of it to none. Her secret was her own and such it would remain. Why should she proclaim to the world the fact that the one whom she loved had chosen another for his wife?

'It is nothing, Teresa,' she said, 'I have not been feeling very well of late, but I expect I shall be all right soon.'

Teresa saw that she did not wish to discuss the matter, and said no more about it, but they talked about other things—talked till late that night, so much had they to say to each other. And Teresa found herself telling Margaret about the lonely girl who had the room across the landing from her own.

'I do hope she gets another job soon,' she said, 'for she seems so unhappy. I don't know why she left her employment, but am afraid it must be something serious—she came home one morning and did not return. Poor Mrs. Doyle is quite upset about it, partly for the sake of Miss Malcolm, and partly, I expect, on the account of her own rent.'

'What did you say the girl's name was?' asked Margaret.

'Nora Malcolm.'

'And where was she employed?'

'I am not sure, but I think it was in the office of some firm of seed merchants.'

'Why—she was down here! She is engaged to Harold Hastings,' cried Margaret. 'Did you not meet him in Dublin?'

'No. I never saw him with her or at the house. How extraordinary! Mrs. Doyle certainly told me that Miss Malcolm had a "nice young man", who used to call and take her out, but that he hadn't been lately. She was thinking that her trouble might have had something to do with him.'

'Oh—I don't think so! Indeed, I am sure they are to be married quite soon—early in the New Year. She was here on a visit to his mother and aunt.'

'But why has he not been to see her lately? And especially when she is in trouble?'

'I can explain that. His mother told me that he is now in Belfast—will probably be there for a fortnight at least. But I am sure she hears from him. It is not about him that she is worrying—I am sure of that.'

'Well, I cannot understand her,' said Teresa.

'If she is to be married in a few months, surely she need not worry about her present position—not having work, and so on. Except she wants to save for her trousseau!'

'I don't know,' said Margaret, rather wearily, 'all I can tell you is that the wedding is fixed for January, and Mrs. Hastings told me yesterday that Harold has written saying that when he returned from Belfast he and Nora must really decide on where they were to live in Dublin. It seems that Nora would like a small house, but he would rather start with a flat.'

'Well, I suppose it will come all right, and I am glad to know what you have told me, as I won't be so anxious now about the girl. And now goodnight, dear—I feel so sleepy.'

CHAPTER XII

HAROLD IS PUZZLED

The week at the farm went by quickly. Teresa enjoyed every moment of it. She went for walks with Michael Conroy and Judy. The old man was much attached to Judy, his small black cocker. Like himself, she was getting old now and her sight was not good, but she could follow him everywhere he went, sticking close to his heels. The days when she could run on in front, racing backwards and forwards, chasing after this and that—those days were gone. But still she seemed to enjoy life in her own way. Although friendly with everyone around, she was recognised as old Conroy's special companion, and alluded to by the farm workers as 'the ould master's dog'.

Teresa was sorry when her holiday was over, but she returned to Dublin, feeling better for the change. The only thing which still worried her was the difference she saw in Margaret. But the girl would not confide in her, so she could do nothing about it. She had spent an evening with Mrs. Hastings and her sister, and they were very interested when she told them that she lived in the same house with Nora. But she said nothing to them about Nora's loss of employment. She did not know whether Nora would have wished her to speak of it to them, and after all, it was none of her business.

The evening that she returned to Rathmines she asked Mrs. Doyle about the girl.

'How is Miss Malcolm—has she got work?' she asked.

'No, indeed she has not,' was the reply, 'and the young man has not returned up either.'

'Oh, that's all right—I can explain about him,' said Teresa, and she told the landlady what she had heard in Wexford.

'Well, that eases me mind a bit as far as Miss Malcolm goes. But of course I might have guessed as much! I never have a good lodger but she goes and leaves me. Look at Mrs. Pender, the lady who was here before you came—the kindness I showed that one—and the short way she went and took me in the end. But that's the world for you! Well, I hope *you* won't be going off and getting married, Miss Mason?'

'No fear of that, Mrs. Doyle,' replied Teresa with a smile.

Nora Tiernan, sitting alone in her room across the hall, heard their talk and laughter and she envied Miss Mason. She was quite old, of course—the forties seem so in the eyes of 'sweet and twenty'—but still Miss Mason seemed happy, there was no doubt about that. And Nora was miserable. Her fruitless search for work, her anxiety about Harold, her sleepless nights and weary days, all combined to make her wretched indeed. Harold would be back any day now, and what excuse was she to make, what plausible story, to account for her leaving Mr. Murphy? Perhaps she had better say she was not feeling well, the work was too heavy and she wanted a lighter job? The work was no harder than it would be in any office. Yet she must say something to account for leaving a place where she had told him that she was happy and content.

However, as things turned out, Harold arrived a few days before he was expected, his business having come to an end. Belfast held no charm for him and he made his way home as soon as possible. There had been something—or a want of something—in Nora's letters which had caused him to feel a bit anxious about her. Was she well? he wondered. Or what was it that caused such a note of coldness, of constraint, in her recent letters—so different from the other gay, delightful ones which he had had from her? Anxious to see her, he made his way to Rathmines, only to be told by Mrs. Doyle that Miss Malcolm was gone out. Harold was surprised, he had thought that at this hour Nora would only be about finished her tea.

'Are you sure she is out?' he asked.

'Oh, quite sure,' replied the landlady, 'although why she goes tramping out at night, after being out all day, beats me!'

'But you see, she is sitting in the office all day,' said Harold, 'and so, no doubt, is glad to go for a walk in the evening.'

'But excuse me, sir, she isn't in the office now—nor hasn't been for over a week.'

'Not been in the office? Is she ill, then? She did not mention in her letters to me that she had left the office.'

'Well, she's not looking too well, and that's a fact, but it's my belief that it's worry that is making her ill. She lost her job suddenly—came home one morning soon after she had gone into work, and has never gone back. Since then she's been looking for another job—but it's not easy to fall into jobs these days, as my son George could tell you—for years now he's been trying to get work and hasn't got it yet.'

But Harold was not interested in George—he was too surprised to hear about Nora.

Harold is Puzzled

'Lost her job,' he exclaimed, 'and she never told me!' Then he added, 'You may not know, but Miss Malcolm is engaged to be married to me. We hope to have the wedding early in January, so she really has no need to worry over anything—in fact, I should be just as glad if she did not take up any other work.'

'Well, then I'm glad to hear your news, sir, and wish you both every happiness,' said Mrs. Doyle, not 'letting on', as she would have said, that she had already heard this news from Miss Mason.

'Thank you, Mrs. Doyle; and now, if you don't mind, I think I will wait a while and see if Miss Malcolm returns.'

'Why, of course, sir. But you will be cold.'

It was then that Harold noticed the fireless grate, so cheerless-looking on this wintry night.

'Did Miss Malcolm not light her fire this evening?' he asked.

'No, she did not, and to tell you the truth, she often goes without it these days. You see she is out near all day, tramping here and there looking for a job, and then at night she goes out again and doesn't be in till late, when she goes to bed.'

'Well, could you light the fire now?' asked Harold.

Mrs. Doyle hesitated. It was not her business to light the tenants' fires. There was another reason, too, for her hesitation. As she knew, Nora had only a few small lumps of coal in the box by the fireplace. She lifted the lid of this box which Nora had covered with chintz and peered within.

'There's not much coal here, sir,' she said.

'Is that all Miss Malcolm has? Has she none in the coal-house?'

'I keep mine in the coal-house,' replied Mrs. Doyle, with dignity, 'the tenants have each their coal-box, but I know that none has been delivered lately for Miss Malcolm.'

Harold was aghast. What did all this mean? Was Nora short of money, or in any trouble, and he did not know of it? Why had she not written to him? Her stupid pride, he supposed.

'Could you lend her some coal?' he asked, putting his hand in his pocket. 'Here are five shillings, just for tonight and your trouble—no, please take it. I will see that Miss Malcolm has a proper supply of coal sent in tomorrow.'

Mrs. Doyle lit a fire—and a good fire, too. It made the room look a different place—bright and cheery.

'That will be nice for her when she comes back,' said Mrs. Doyle, 'and how pleased she will be to see you, sir, when she did not expect you.'

'Yes—I got home sooner than I expected,' he replied.

When Mrs. Doyle had left him, he sat alone by the fire. The minutes went by and he wondered what could be keeping Nora. Had she gone to the pictures? But he knew she seldom went to them—unlike most modern girls. Yet what could be keeping her so long?

It was a cold, blustery night, the rain beating against the window, a night upon which most people would have preferred their fireside to being out in such weather. Mrs. Doyle looked in presently, made up the fire and seemed disposed for a chat, but finding Harold unresponsive, she departed to her basement quarters to await the return of George from the pictures and to prepare a nice supper for him. She wished Miss Mason had been in, she would have liked to tell her about Mr. Hastings, but Teresa was spending the evening with friends and would not be back until late.

It was after ten o'clock when at last Harold heard a latch-key turn in the front door, and a moment afterwards Nora entered the room.

But was this Nora—this haggard, pale-faced girl, with lagging step and listless manner, who gazed before her with desolate, unseeing eyes, until they lighted upon Harold? She gave a little cry then and almost seemed to shrink back—away from him as if afraid.

'Nora!' he exclaimed. 'What is it—what is the matter? You are ill. Why did you not tell me?'

He went forward, putting his arms around her, drawing her towards the fire, taking off her coat so wet from the heavy rain.

'My darling, what does this mean? Are you in trouble—and never told me?'

Desperately she tried to rally, to smile, to be like the girl he had known. She must not arouse his suspicions, must not let him think that anything was really wrong. Oh, why had she not known that he would call that night?

'Sit at the fire,' he was saying, 'and I will make you some tea— I am a great hand at that!—the kettle is boiling on the hob as you may see. Or would you rather have some hot milk?'

She tried then to laugh, but it was a sorry attempt at mirth.

'What a fuss you are making,' she said, 'I do not want anything, thank you. I have been to see some friends and had tea with them.'

He looked at her, surprised, puzzled. Had it been anyone else but Nora he would not have believed her, but she had always seemed to be the very essence of truth, so why should he doubt her now? Yet

Harold is Puzzled

she was so wet, looking as if she had been out for hours in the rain. Why had she not taken a tram? They passed the end of the road.

'Where do your friends live?' he asked. 'It must be a good distance away.'

'Oh, yes—over the North side,' she replied. After all, what did it matter now how many lies she told, she had already told so many. Her one wish was to keep him in ignorance of the real state of affairs. But his next words showed her that he already knew something.

'So you have left Murphy's?'

'Yes. How did you know?

'Mrs. Doyle told me.'

'I see. Yes, I left as I have hopes of a much better job—besides, I was tired and sick of Murphy's—I never liked it.'

'I thought you were quite happy there. But there is no need for you to worry about getting other work now—is there, Nora? Now that our marriage is so near I want you to be free of all work or trouble. You are not looking well either. Why not go and stay with my people for a while? Mother would be delighted I know, and it would do you all the good in the world. You want a change. Won't you think about it?'

'Oh, yes, I'll think about it—thank you very much.'

But there was something in her manner which puzzled Harold. This was not the Nora whom he had known—she was almost like a stranger. That something must have happened while he was away he felt sure. But she would say nothing—he knew that. Yet he was determined to get to the bottom of it all, although he said nothing of his resolve to Nora. For her he could only feel a great pity. She looked so cold and wet, so unhappy, for her would-be laughter and her attempts to be light-hearted, did not deceive him. However, he must go now, it was time she got to bed—how tired she looked.

'I will go now, dear,' he said, 'you will want your rest. May I come round tomorrow?'

'Oh, yes—tomorrow,' she said. And he saw that she was eager for him to leave her.

'All right,' he said, 'I'll be here about half-past five and we can go and have tea somewhere, and do a show afterwards—will that suit you?'

'Yes, of course, and thanks so much. You must forgive me for being a bit dull tonight, but I'm rather tired. I'll be all right tomorrow.'

Harold went away then. But he thought of her when he reached his own place. He could not forget her face—her hopeless expression—when she had first entered the room, before she saw him. What could be the matter? He possessed the legal mind to a great degree and was seldom wrong in his deductions. Now he was certain that Nora's trouble must be in some way connected with her position in the office of Murphy and Co. This seemed quite plain to him. She had said that she hoped for a better job, but why had she left where she was employed before the other post had materialised? And why should she have troubled about another job at all when she was to be married so soon?

Harold's mind was made up before he went to bed that night. He would go and see Mr. Murphy in the morning. An interview with him should put matters clear—put him in possession of the plain facts of the case.

CHAPTER XIII

NEMESIS

Nora had been so tired, so weary that she had gone to bed at once when Harold left her. She had not thought that she would be able to sleep, but to her surprise she fell asleep almost at once and never awoke until she heard Teresa Mason going out, as usual, to seven o'clock Mass.

Nora lay in bed, thinking over things. There was no hurry about getting up, she had given up the practice of daily Mass for a good while now. She was no hypocrite, whatever else she might be, and she would not keep up a pretence of religion when she had surrounded herself with lies and deceit. She now cared for nothing but just to keep Harold's love, to be able to so arrange matters that he should remain in ignorance of her real parentage—might believe, as his mother had done—that she was the daughter of a poor but honest commercial traveller who had died respectably from natural causes. Ever since Mrs. Hastings had told her how Harold felt towards the family of the man who had robbed his father and been the cause of his death, she had been more anxious than ever that her real name should not become known to him. She was foolish, indeed, to try and keep this knowledge from him. Had she but considered the matter from a more sensible angle, her common-sense would have told her that the truth was almost sure to come out, sooner or later. But her love made her reckless, and she still clung to the belief that once married to Harold he would forgive her deception. Had she but known him better, she would have realised that the exact opposite would have been the case.

This morning she felt better after her night's rest—it was some time since she had slept so well. The day, too, was bright and fine, although cold, and in consequence things began to look more hopeful. After all, why should not everything turn out all right? Who was going to tell Harold the facts? He was not likely to meet either Rose Malone or Mr. Murphy—and who else would tell him? The Derwents, of course, might think that she should tell Harold everything, but they were safe in America, and she would probably be married long before they returned. Harold loved her deeply—she knew that. How delighted he had been to see her last night, and how upset when he saw how wet and tired she was. She was sure he had suspected nothing—and why should he ever do so? She had only to be very careful and all would be well.

She wished that she had known of his coming last night. Had she expected him she would not have gone for that long tramp in the rain, she would have been at home, and have tried to look her best for him.

Well, he was coming this evening and she would show him a different Nora from the one he had seen last night. She would have lots of time to make both the room and herself quite pretty in his honour. There was only one advertisement about which she had to go and see that morning. It was for a typist in the office of a wholesale manufacturer on the Quays, and immediately after her breakfast, Nora set off for the place. She hardly cared now whether she got the job or not, so excited did she feel about Harold's return—so different altogether from the tired, weary girl of the night before. So much does one good night's sleep do for us at times. Still she would like to get work, not only because it would look well if she did so, but also because she wanted money for her trousseau. Not that she would be able to afford very much in the way of clothes, but her pride would not allow her to accept anything from Harold before they were married, and she did want a new frock at least, and if possible a hat and coat. Underclothes— and most things—were cheap enough in those days just before the war; little did the brides then dream that the days would come when they would have to pay unheard of prices and also produce coupons for any clothes they wished to buy. Nora had but a few pounds put by; it was not easy to keep oneself and save out of a salary of thirty shillings a week, and neither by character nor upbringing was Nora of the saving type.

The result of her interview this morning was the same as usual. She had been employed previously—but could give no reference from her late employer. They were afraid she would not suit.

But today she did not mind the disappointment so much, she was too glad at the thought of seeing Harold, of going out with him for an evening's amusement, to worry over what, after all, she had expected. She had begun to realise that employment for her was out of the question. Should she do as Harold wished, and stay for a while with his mother? If only Mrs. Hastings or her sister would not ask her any more questions about her past. And somehow she did not think that they would do so now. Mrs. Hastings had so quietly accepted her story, never seeming to doubt it for a moment. She might do worse than go there for a few weeks—it would be a change. But she would have much preferred another job—something which she could keep for a month or so—until just before her wedding—she wanted so badly to earn money. Her summer holiday had taken most of her small savings—how could she buy what she needed?

However, let each day take care of itself! Today she would forget her troubles—put them behind her as if they had never been. She was not the daughter of John Tiernan—but of that poor commercial traveller, so honest and decent—and she was going to be married to the man she loved and who loved her.

Before she went to Rathmines, she went to a hairdresser and had her hair shampooed and waved. She also bought muffins—which Harold liked so much—and cakes, for she had decided to give him tea cosily by the fire in her room before they went out. Her mid-day meal was but tea and bread and butter, for she was not hungry—too excited to eat. The hours were long in passing before it was time to set the table for the tea. She had given her room a great 'tidying up,' and by half-past five the kettle was boiling on the hob, the muffins toasted and ready in a covered dish, and herself and the room in festive attire, breathing a welcome in every detail.

But at that hour he had not come. Nor had he arrived at a quarter to six—or even six o'clock.

Nora at first had not been uneasy—Harold had just been delayed by some last-minute business. But as time went on and half-past six chimed from the Rathmines Town Hall, she could not but wonder what was keeping him. The muffins would be hard, the kettle had nearly boiled away. She went out to refill it from the tap at the sink which was a few steps down from the hall, and it was as she was doing so that a quick knock came to the front door. She ran to open it—kettle in hand. This must be Harold. No—only a messenger boy with a letter. 'Miss Malcolm?' he asked. 'Yes—that's right.'

As Nora took it, she saw that the address was in Harold's handwriting. So, she thought, Mr. Grey wanted him for something. But perhaps he might be coming later, and had sent a line to let her know. Going back to her room, she put the kettle down and opened the letter.

It began at once without any form of address. And these are the words she read:

'I know all. Your lies and deceit are now revealed to me, and I know you as Nora Tiernan, the daughter of my greatest enemy—the man who ruined my beloved father, and was the cause of his early death—the cause of my dear mother's poverty—and my own. You have wilfully deceived me from the very beginning of our friendship. You told lies to my mother about your parentage—you dare not speak the truth. I cannot write much to you, for when I think of the girl whom I had imagined you to be—so kind, so honest, so *true*—and now understand the truth about Nora Tiernan, the bitterness of death is mine. I have no more to say, no more is needed. In those words, "I know all", all is said between us—and all is ended. I pray God that I may never see your false face again, and I thank Him that the truth was shown to me before it was too late.

Harold Hastings'

For a few moments Nora stood there, trying to read the words which kept dancing in some queer way before her eyes. Then as their meaning became clear to her, she gave a little moan and groped for a chair and sat down because her legs seemed no longer able to support her. So he knew all. All was over, everything finished between them. She would never again see his dear face, hear his beloved voice.

Her thoughts went back to last night, to his tender care for her, his wish to do something for her comfort. 'I am a great hand at making tea!'—the homely, dear words, she could hear him speaking them. And now she would never have him to tea—never again—never be able to make tea for him or let him make it for her. Her eyes went to the kettle, to the tea-pot, the pretty cosy, the muffins, so lovingly prepared for him. But all was over, he had written. And he never wanted to see her face—her false face again.

How long she sat there she did not know. When at last she roused herself the fire had gone out, the muffins were hard and cold in their covered dish. It was night. Night, too—black night—in Nora's heart.

CHAPTER XIV
CHRISTMAS EVE

Christmas Eve in Dublin. Crowds hurrying along the streets intent on last-minute shopping; crowds thronging the churches for Confession; crowds, rushing for bus or tram—crowds everywhere. Good humoured crowds, all of them, imbued with that spirit of goodwill and kindness, which it is a pity we cannot keep with us all the year round.

But Nora Tiernan, as she walked along Grafton Street on her way home to Rathmines, at five o'clock on this Christmas Eve, making her way mechanically through the jostling, merry crowds, hardly saw any of them. The shops, so gay and pretty, had no attraction for her, she had neither the wish nor the money to purchase anything. One penny was all that remained in her purse after she had paid her rent that morning, had bought a loaf, a quarter of a pound of margarine, and two ounces of tea. This would constitute her Christmas fare, leaving her the penny.

Somehow, she did not seem to mind, feeling more or less indifferent about it all. For months now she had been looking for work and had looked in vain. It was always the same. No references—no work. Had she been in better health and spirits she would have tried for some other kind of work—even gone as a maid—anything to keep body and soul together. But she was so weary of it all that nothing seemed to matter now. She was in poor health physically from lack of proper food, and today she felt almost ill, so that she walked with queer, jerky movements like an automaton. She had no definite business out of doors on this Christmas Eve, no shopping, neither had she any intention of going to Confession. She had simply come out in an effort to get warm by walking. But she was still cold as she turned her face towards Rathmines, and it was no wonder, for it was a day of severe frost, and both her shoes and coat were thin. In St. Stephen's Green the ponds were frozen over, and as she passed the gates she heard shouts of laughter from the skaters. Great weather for those people who were warmly clad and well fed—not so grand for the poor. Wearily Nora kept on her way, walking along Harcourt Street, her eyes staring blankly in front of her, seeing no one. Suddenly she was startled by hearing a voice she recognised, exclaiming: 'Nora Malcolm—is it you! How are you?'

She lifted her eyes and saw Mary Gilfoyle standing in front of her, holding out her hand with a smile.

'Happy Christmas!' she was saying. Then as she saw Nora's face more clearly, she asked with a swift change of voice, 'But are you not well? You look ill.'

There was no reply, the girl to whom she spoke just looked at her as if they had never met before, then passed on her way, leaving Mary Gilfoyle staring after her.

'Oh, poor girl!' she murmured, 'how wretched she looks!'

Mary felt as if she should have followed Nora, tried to make her speak. But she was laden with parcels, and just at that moment the tram hove in sight which would take her to Rathgar where she would get the Whitechurch bus. But she spoke about the meeting later that evening as she sat with her mother and Anne, having tea in the delightful old parlour of Lilac Tree House. The garden was now ice-bound, and away to the back the Dublin mountains towered in loveliness, standing like snow-covered sentinels guarding the city at their feet.

'I met Nora Malcolm today,' said Mary. She could never think of Nora by her real name, she had been so used to calling her by the other—although now, thanks to Rose Malone, the whole office knew her story.

'Nora Malcolm!' exclaimed Anne.

'Yes—in Harcourt Street while I was waiting for the tram. She looks so bad—really ill—and poor and shabby. I felt so sorry for her.'

'But did you not speak to her?' asked her mother.

'Of course, but she would not reply. She just stared at me as if I were a stranger, and passed on.'

'I am anxious about that girl,' said Mrs. Gilfoyle.

'I suppose she has not been able to get work, and I wonder how she is managing to live.'

'I think she is having a bad time right enough,' said Mary, 'and I wish she had spoken. Another time I would have followed her, tried to get her to speak, but I was so rushed and had such a lot of parcels. I was tired, too, and just didn't bother. But I'm sorry now.'

'Do you know where she lives?'

'Yes—at least I know where she lived when she was at Murphy's. I don't know if she is still there, of course. She lived then in Chesnut Avenue, Rathmines.'

'Well, I think you should go there and see if she is living there still. We might be able to help her.'

'I suppose you don't think she took those things from the office—do you?' asked Anne.

'No—I do not. Her manner at the time seemed strange to me, but when Rose Malone told me all about her father after she had left, I felt sure that it had been just pure worry on her part. You know, mother, I wrote to her several times asking if I might go and see her, but she did not reply.'

'Well, I think you should go now.'

'Why not go yourself, mother?' asked Anne. 'If anyone could get round her—it would be you.'

Mrs. Gilfoyle smiled.

'All right,' she said. 'I will try to see her on St. Stephen's Day. Perhaps I might persuade her to come to us for a little while—it would do her good.'

At that very moment the subject of their conversation was sitting alone in her fireless room. Her last bit of coal was gone, her last penny had gone in the gas to make a cup of tea. And now she was sitting in lonely misery on Christmas Eve. Mrs. Doyle had looked in to ask how she was; the landlady was a bit anxious about this tenant of hers. Her knowledge of life, the memory of many tenants who had come and gone—some of them owing her rent—made her suspect that all was not right with Miss Malcolm. The girl was so unlike herself, too, and had become so pale and delicate. Mrs. Doyle had spoken of her anxiety to Teresa Mason earlier in the evening, had asked her to try and see Miss Mason—'just to let me know what you think of her, poor thing. It's my belief she's hungry.'

'Oh, surely not Mrs. Doyle! And this is Christmas Eve!'

'Well, perhaps not—but I know that she has been disposing of a lot of things lately—and she valued them I know. Still one must eat—although it's not much *she* has to eat, if you ask me.'

After she had finished her own tea, Teresa put some cake on a plate, and going across the landing, knocked, but there was no answer. It was evident that Nora did not mean to open the door. Teresa had hoped that as it was Christmas she might have done so, but as she knew from Mrs. Doyle that Nora was still in her room, it was plain to be seen that the girl wished to be left alone. Teresa would not intrude where she was not wanted, and returned to her own room, still carrying the plate of cake and feeling very disappointed.

So the hours passed and Nora sat there in the dark—alone.

She was thinking of the past few months and all that had happened; her meeting with Harold, her fear and hesitation about telling him the truth, then his mother's disclosure to herself, which seemed to make it impossible that she should ever tell him. And then he had heard the truth from others. Heard it and cast her off for ever. Over and over again she asked herself the question—if she had told him everything in the beginning would it have made any difference? She did not know. Never would know now. And so she was left desolate and alone. Not only alone but penniless as well—really penniless, not just in the sense of meaning that she was badly off. She was absolutely without a penny on this eve of Christmas. It had been only by pawning or selling any little articles of value which she still possessed, that she had managed to exist at all.

And now what was she to do? She could not remain any longer with Mrs. Doyle for she would not have rent for the coming week. She had never had to ask her to wait for her rent and never would do so. Often she had gone hungry in order to pay the ten shillings a week for her room. She realised now that she should have moved to cheaper quarters before this, but even if she had got a room at five shillings a week, it would not have made much difference. No—there was nothing now that she could do. She had come to the end of her resources. Hungry and cold, wretched in body and mind, she sat there listening to the hours striking from the Town Hall clock.

Had she had a little bit of comfort around her, a bright fire, a cup of tea, she would not have felt so desolate; but weary as she was, tired bodily and mentally, she could see no gleam of hope anywhere.

Suddenly the bells rang out to welcome in Christmas morning. Plainly heard in the silence of the starry night, they rang their joyful message to all mankind—'Peace on earth to men of goodwill.'

Beautiful bells are those of St. Patrick's, coming down to us from the days when Catholics worshipped in our old cathedral. Christ Church joined with them, and over all Dublin City their music was wafted.

Nora heard them, they roused her from her apathy, but far from bringing her any comfort or hope, they seemed but to accentuate her misery. Christmastide—goodwill—what did it all mean to her? Nothing, and worse than nothing. She would not allow her thoughts to go back to those happy, innocent days, now past and gone—the time when Christmas had meant happiness indeed to her, with her beloved daddy in her dear old home. Now she could think only of the present and its load of misery. Was there no way out of it all? How she wished she had been a Roman of old, then she could have opened a vein in her arm and drifted quietly away to where the grim Ferryman sat awaiting her. But she would not know how to do anything like that. But there was the gas. How often had she read in the newspapers about people putting an end to their lives by gas. But here again she was helpless. She had not a penny for the gas even if her gas ring would have been effectual. Oh—the irony of it! Compelled to stay on this earth for the want of a few pence. And yet her poor father, even while about to take is own life, had described the act as 'the coward's way out'. And the Church taught that self-murder was a mortal sin—she would have lost her soul for ever.

She was mad to have thought of such a thing—she hoped God would forgive her. How cold and hungry she was, yet not so much hungry as faint. Perhaps if she took a slice of bread and margarine she would feel better. The little tea she had must be kept for the morning. She rose from her seat, cramped and cold, and started to grope her way to the switch near the door. How giddy she was! Would she ever reach the door, ever be able to turn on the light? Ah, here it was! She reached forth her hand to switch on the light, but before she could do so, a deadly faintness overcame her and she pitched forward and knew no more.

Teresa Mason had not gone to bed. She always sat up to listen to the joybells, and now she was sitting by the fire in her dressing-gown. The house was very quiet. Mrs. Doyle, downstairs in the basement, had evidently retired to bed; whether the handsome George was at home yet or not, Teresa did not know.

Pat Doyle and his family were fast asleep, they were all going to first Mass at six o'clock in the morning, and had had a tiring day with their excited youngsters—and little Miss Moran and her pet dog were also in bed and asleep.

'I may as well go to bed myself,' thought Teresa, as the bells died away and silence was all around. A silence which was broken suddenly by a queer sound—it was like a thud, as if something heavy had fallen somewhere. And it seemed to come from across the landing—from Nora Malcolm's room. What could it be? Could something have happened to that poor girl?

She opened her door quietly and went softly across the landing to that other door upon which she had knocked in vain earlier in the night. She listened, but there was not a sound. Yet the silence had something queer about it which Teresa did not like. She resolved to open the door—Nora could not kill her anyhow! Quietly but firmly she turned the handle. But the door only opened very little way, there was something stopping it, something which prevented it from opening wide. Teresa could reach the switch from where she stood, and the next moment she could see the room and that which had prevented her from entering it. Poor little Nora lay on the floor, right across the threshold, motionless and still. For a second Teresa had a fear that she was dead, but a hasty examination told her that the girl had only fainted. A swift glance also showed her the empty grate, the cold chill of the room—so bare of every comfort.

The first thing was to get the poor girl warm. Teresa had no wish to rouse Mrs. Doyle, and was sure that Nora would not wish her to do so either. She was strong, knew, too, how to lift unconscious people, so in a few minutes she had carried Nora across the landing to her own room—and she was not a heavy weight. There she laid her on the bed, loosened her clothes, wrapped her in blankets, place a hot-water bag to her feet. She made up a good fire then and watched to see if the girl would come round. And soon she was rewarded by seeing a tinge of colour come into the pale face. After a moment Nora opened her eyes and stared at Teresa.

'Why—where am I?' she asked.

'In my room dear,' replied Teresa with a smile.

'You fainted, and I wanted to get you warm. You feel better now—don't you?'

Nora nodded while she looked around the room, so bright and cosy, above all so warm—such a contrast to her own cheerless one.

Teresa said no more, but she warmed some milk and gave it to her. She noticed how eagerly the girl drank it, her trembling hands raised the cup to her lips and she drank greedily. A sudden suspicion came to Teresa. Could this girl be hungry as well as cold?

'You liked that?' she asked. 'I am glad you were able to take it, and now I want you to have some porridge—just a little, I have it here, cooked and all.'

Nora needed no coaxing, she was too weak to say much, but she was very glad of the nourishment, but so tired, so exhausted, that she fell asleep almost before she had finished it.

Teresa watched beside her for a little while, but she continued to sleep, so presently the other made up a bed for herself on the sofa, for she would not disturb Nora. 'I may as well try and get a little sleep before it's time for Mass,' she said. And very soon she, too, slept.

CHAPTER XV

AN INVITATION

Nora was still sleeping when Teresa slipped out to early Mass that Christmas morning, but on her return the girl was awake.

'Well, how do you feel this morning?' asked Teresa as she kissed her. 'Happy Christmas, dear!'

Nora said nothing. She was still feeling weak, but she did not like being there in Miss Mason's room.

'I am sorry to be such a trouble to you,' she said presently, as she watched Teresa putting a match to the fire which she had set before going out.

'Oh, my dear girl—you are no trouble at all—don't think that for a moment! I was only too glad to be able to help you last night. I heard you fall, you know.'

'Yes—I must have got faint.'

'Well, don't try to remember anything about it just yet—wait until we have had our breakfast. No—don't attempt to get up, you are to have your breakfast in bed.'

She put the kettle on the gas, also the pan with some rashers. These were soon sizzling away with very appetising odour, and presently Nora was eating—and enjoying—such a breakfast as she had not known for some time. Teresa, as she watched her eating, guessed that the girl must have been half starved for days, and she blamed herself bitterly for not having tried to help her before now. But Nora would not have let her, she realised that. As long as she could have managed to hold out on her own, she would never have given in. And what had happened to Harold Hastings? It was quite plain that they had parted.

But now, comfort and kindness did what hardship could not accomplish. The good breakfast, the comfortable room and bright fire, Teresa's real kindness—all combined to break down the wall of icy reserve which Nora had built around herself. She was soon talking to Teresa as she had never talked to anyone else.

'But, my dear, why did you not speak to me before?' asked Teresa. 'I am sure I could have got something for you to do. And in any case, a trouble shared is a trouble halved—don't you know that? But now you will have to take it easy for a while—try and build up your strength before you think of work.'

An Invitation

Nora gulped down her last bit of pride.

'But I have no money,' she confessed, 'not a penny—*really* not one penny—my last one went in the gas yesterday. I cannot buy food and I will not be able to pay my rent for next week.'

'Oh—you must not worry,' replied Teresa, cheerily. 'You will just be my guest for the present—now please! It is Christmas time, and after all you can pay me back later if you wish. But if we cannot help each other on this great Day—it's a queer thing! So now, don't worry, and remember that when things look blackest, they generally take a turn for the better.'

The kind voice, the cheery tones with their message of hope, brought the relief of tears to Nora. Teresa let her have her cry out, knowing that it would do her good. When the girl had recovered her self-control, she said to her: 'Now, my dear, if you feel able would you not like to go to Mass? And then when you come back you must help me to cook the lovely chicken which was sent to me from the country.'

But she did not mention that it had been sent by Margaret Conroy from the farm. She had not told Nora that she knew the Hastings family or anyone in that part of the country. She was afraid that if Nora knew this, it might cause some restraint on her part and this was what Teresa did not want.

It was early the following afternoon, just when the two friends—as they really were now—had finished their mid-day dinner, that Mrs. Gilfoyle knocked at the door of No. 17 Chesnut Avenue. Mrs. Doyle answered it. The landlady had been told that Miss Malcolm had been taken ill in the night and that Miss Mason had looked after her, and Mrs, Doyle was glad to see that the two were quite friendly now, sitting in Miss Mason's room, having their meal together.

'Miss Malcolm?' she repeated now, in reply to Mrs. Gilfoyle. 'Oh, yes, she is here and at home at the moment. But she is not very well and is with Miss Mason, who is looking after her—she is another tenant.'

'Do you think I might see Miss Malcolm?'

'I will ask.'

Mrs. Doyle gave a knock at Teresa's door and announced that there was a lady to see Miss Malcolm. Mrs. Gilfoyle, standing on the mat just inside the front door, heard Nora say in a frightened voice:

'Oh, who can it be? I don't want to see anyone.'

'Will I see her for you?'

'Yes—please do!'

Teresa found Mrs. Gilfoyle waiting in the hall. She liked her on first sight, she seemed so calm and quite, such a spirit of serenity enveloped her.

'You wished to see Miss Malcolm?'

'Yes—if I may. I am sorry to hear she is not very well, but I should like to see her if possible. I knew her and her family years ago, and it was to ask her to come to us for a visit that I came today. My daughters and myself live at Whitechurch. Gilfoyle is my name. Perhaps you have heard Miss Malcolm speak of us?'

'No—but then it is only since she has been ill that we have spoken much to each other. I should have been glad to have been friendly with her before this, but she is rather reserved, as I suppose you know.'

'Yes, I know. Well now, don't you think that a change to mountain air, with rest and quiet, would help her?'

'I know that it would, and I should be delighted if she would go. But you had better ask her yourself, Mrs. Gilfoyle.'

'Thank you, Miss——'

'Mason is my name.'

'Then, Miss Mason, would you mind very much if I asked you to leave me alone with Nora Malcolm for a little while?'

Teresa was surprised, but agreed at once. 'This is my room,' she said. 'Here is an old friend to see you, Nora.'

She ushered Mrs. Gilfoyle into the room then went across to Nora's room across the landing, and waited there until she heard Mrs. Gilfoyle come out.

When Mrs. Gilfoyle saw Nora, she was really distressed to see such a change in her. She had become so pale and thin, seeming, too, like one who had lost her youth suddenly, so worn and haggard did she appear. Mrs. Gilfoyle could remember her as a happy young girl in her home in Rathgar before tragedy had come to her life. When she had met her again on that evening when she had come to Lilac Tree House, the girl had been so upset at recognising Mrs. Gilfoyle that all her brightness and gaiety had fled for the moment, leaving her crushed and anxious. But never had she looked so badly as she did now.

'My dear child—I am so sorry you are not well!' exclaimed Mrs. Gilfoyle. 'What has been the matter at all? And are you getting better now?'

An Invitation

'I am all right, thank you,' was the rather cold reply.

'I do not think that you are—far from it indeed,' was the other's reply. The older woman seated herself as she spoke, taking a chair opposite to Nora, so that she could see her well. 'Now you must listen to me,' she went on, 'and do not interrupt until I have finished. First of all, Mary told me that she had met you on Christmas Eve, but that you would not speak to her. She felt this very much. You see, she wished to talk to you—to ask you to come and see us, although you never answered her letters. We are not like other people whom you may know. All your sad history is known to me, and I knew and loved your mother, and always thought a lot of your father. I am sure he was not in his right mind when he took his own life. Now you are not to brood over these things. You have been through a bad time, I can see that, and you have got run down with care and anxiety. So now we want you—my girls and myself—to come to us at Lilac Tree House for a good long visit, until you get strong again and able to work. Will you come?'

'But Mary thinks I stole those things from the office. I know she does.'

'Indeed, you are mistaken—she thinks nothing of the sort. But she felt rather sore because you would not confide in her that time when you were in trouble. She is only anxious to see you and be friends with you again. Now won't you come to us? A very warm welcome awaits you.'

For a few moments Nora was silent. Had she been asked to go and stay with the Gilfoyles a few days ago, she would have refused at once. But somehow, she had been strangely softened by Teresa's kindness. She was feeling better, too, with the comfort and the warmth—so different from the cold misery which she had endured for weeks past. She knew that she must find work in order to live—and to do this she would have to be strong and well. She did not wish to be a burden on Teresa who had only her salary to live upon, and she must return to duty in a few days when the holidays were over, and then she herself would be left alone all through the long, weary, winter days. At Lilac Tree House she would not be alone, she would have this kindly woman to speak to—to consult with. Surely in the peace of the Dublin hills she would get better, her strength would return to her and she would be able to work again. She would feel better able to fight the world after a rest. Surely there must be some work which she could get.

She raised her eyes to where the other sat watching her anxiously. 'Thank you, Mrs. Gilfoyle,' she said. 'I will come if you really wish it.'

Nora went to Lilac Tree House a few days later, and there, in the peace and quiet, the homelike atmosphere, she grew stronger day by day. She became very fond of the two girls, but it was their mother who won her real love and gratitude. To her she opened her heart, making full confession, telling her everything— how she had deceived and lied to Harold and his mother, how he had discovered the truth from someone else, and of the terrible letter which he had written then—the words of which were engraved for ever on her heart. Mrs. Gilfoyle listened with quiet sympathy, saying little; she understood how greatly the girl had been tempted and could feel for her only a deep pity. This was not the time to be hard. Instead she spoke words of love and sympathy, holding Nora's hand in her own.

'My dear child,' she said, 'you have suffered greatly—and are still suffering. Perhaps God has called upon you to make reparation for your father's sins. Take all this in the right spirit, offer all your troubles and sufferings for those sins—and for your own sins also. Just leave yourself in Our Lord's Hands and see what He will do for you.'

Nora was silent. she was thinking that the Hand of God was laid very heavily upon her. Perhaps she deserved it, but she could not feel resigned to His Will yet. Mrs. Gilfoyle knew this, but although she was anxious about the girl's spiritual state she did not wish to 'preach' too much.

But the influence of such a truly Catholic household could not fail to react upon Nora; she had always been more or less careless with regard to religious matters, and especially so of late when Heaven itself seemed turned against her, but seeing the daily lives of those at Lilac Tree House, noting the influence which their Faith had upon their lives, she could not but compare their Rule of Life with her own—and the difference was great.

The weather continued dry and frosty, and Nora was soon able to take walks around the country roads, making her way slowly up the hills, so beautiful now, still covered with snow.

One day she went up Tibradden to the very spot where Harold had asked her to be his wife on that August day which now seemed a hundred years ago. Then it had been summer, now it was winter—

it was winter in her heart too. Standing there, she recalled those happy hours, their gay little picnic, the hungry dog, her sudden panic when Harold asked her questions, her resolve not to think of such matters for the moment, their cycle ride together through lovely Whitechurch, talking of the beauty of Dublin. And now it was all over—her love dream shattered, happiness gone. But there remained Life—and it must be faced. She would have to get work soon for she could not stay much longer with the Gilfoyles. Kind as they were to her, her pride would not allow her to remain indefinitely at Lilac Tree House.

But it so happened that in February Mrs. Gilfoyle had a severe attack of influenza. Her daughters were very anxious about her as she was far from strong. Nora was of great assistance to Anne, and Mary was delighted to know she was able to help her sister who could not have managed the house and poultry, and attend on the sick woman all by herself, but Nora being there eased her mind, so that she need not give up her office work, which otherwise she might have had to do. Mrs. Gilfoyle was slow recovering her strength, and winter had passed and spring come before she was able to get about as usual. Spring had come early that year, the ice melted in the garden of Lilac Tree House, and the snow melted from the mountain heights.

And from Nora's heart the ice melted too. April found her strong and well again, more like the Nora of old before tragedy had come to her. Her visit to the Gilfoyles had now lasted for over three months, and she was almost like one of the family. She had returned to her religious duties too, going to the Sacraments each week. Peace was gradually coming to her soul.

Anne and Mary wished her to stay with them for the summer, but she felt it was time to face the world again—to look for work, and Mrs. Gilfoyle agreed with her—she knew it would be best for the girl herself. 'But you will stay here until you get work,' she said, 'or if you like, when you do get work, maybe you will stay with us altogether, you could be into town every day with Mary—you would like that?'

Would she not? If only she could get a job! She agreed to stay in the meantime, and was glad to do so, for she had no money for rent or food, and had already been obliged to accept small loans for any little things which she needed.

Then began the weary search for work, going into town day after day, answering advertisements, calling on this person and on that. Very tiring days for Nora—these lovely days of April. From Anne she got the loan of her bicycle, as she had no money for the bus, and hated having to ask for it. She felt so bitterly having to accept money from these kind people who had already done so much for her—even although she knew that it was always given with ungrudging generosity. How she prayed and hoped for work—any kind of work which would enable her to live, no matter how poorly. She sometimes wished that she might become rich—win the Sweep or something like that—so that she might be able to repay a little of what she owed to these dear people who had been such real friends in need to her. Not that they ever thought of such a thing, and of course their kindness—their goodness—could never be repaid.

And now she could not even get work, no one wanted a typist who had been previously employed but had no reference. Would she have to tell more lies—say she had not been employed before—was looking for a job for the first time? No! She would not do that, she was finished with lies and deceit for all time. She knew now that the truth was always best. Let cynics like Pilate ask: 'What is Truth?' Nora Tiernan knew what it was—what it stood for—and she would respect it.

The weeks passed and May was with them—Our Lady's lovely month. The trees from which Lilac Tree House got its name were in full bloom, the garden ablaze with spring flowers. How happy Nora could have been, she often thought, if only she had had a job, cycling in and out to town with Mary, coming home in the lovely evenings to the beauty of the dear little house where welcome always waited.

But no job came her way, and as time went on Nora began to lose heart. In despair she determined to try for any kind of work. Why not go as a nursemaid? She was fond of children and not afraid of hard work. She did not find it easy to get her friends to agree to this, but at length she prevailed upon Mrs. Gilfoyle to give her a reference as being good at housework, and strictly honest, and so on. So Nora departed one morning to call at several houses where a nursemaid was wanted.

CHAPTER XVI

AN OLD FENIAN GOES HOME

> What to me is the summer's pride?
> Or Spring's young verdure, daisy-pied?
> Winter is in my bones and hair,
> Dead leaves are round me everywhere.
> I am crinkled up like a withered bough
> And the years are heavy upon my brow ...
> O! I long for rest in the goodly clay
> With the dear dead roses of yesterday
>   — *Hugh MacCartan.*

Old Michael Conroy lay dying. He had only taken to his bed the previous day, and to the eyes of his great-grandson there seemed to be nothing the matter with him—he appeared just as usual. He had told Pat to send for the priest, and Father O'Connor had come and administered the Last Sacraments. He did not think the old man was in danger of death, but of course at that age one had to be careful, so the Last Sacraments were given to Michael, and he lay quietly, with wrinkled, toil-worn hands folded in prayer, a look of great peace upon his parchment-like face. One thing more he wanted—to see Teresa.

'I would like to see her before I die—I want to say goodbye to her.'

'But, grand-dad, you are not ill. Why do you talk of dying?'

'Don't let ye argue with me, but send at once for Teresa Mason. Send at once for her, boy—tell her to come as quickly as possible. I may not live to see her if she doesn't hurry.'

'I suppose I had better wire, as he makes such a fuss about it,' said Pat afterwards to Margaret, 'but I don't for the life of me see what the old man wants with her in such a hurry. As to dying—I don't see any difference in him—do you?'

'Well—I don't know,' replied Margaret, 'he doesn't seem ill, but he is not like himself—there is something strange about him.'

'All right, I'll send the wire,' and Pat started to cycle to the post office.

Teresa arrived that night, having just managed to catch a bus. She found the old man sitting up in bed, a knitted woollen jacket round his shoulders, a huge nightcap on his head. Judy lay at the foot, and barked furiously until it dawned upon her who Teresa was, when she wagged her tail in apology. Michael's face was yellow and wrinkled as parchment, but the dim old eyes lit up with pleasure when he saw Teresa.

'So ye have come to say goodbye to an old man—God bless you for that! And I want to talk with ye, but let ye first go down and have some tea, ye must be wanting it after your journey.'

'Won't you have a cup, too?' asked Teresa, knowing his fondness for tea.

'No—not now—mebbe later. Let ye go now and get something to eat and drink and then come back to me, for I want to talk to ye.'

Teresa found Pat and Margaret waiting for her with a substantial meal ready.

'Well, how do you think he is?' asked Pat.

'I don't know,' she replied. 'He does not seem ill—yet he is not like himself someway.'

'That is just what I thought,' said Margaret.

'Has he had the doctor?' asked Teresa.

'No—he would not let us send for him—said he could do no good, so why trouble him?'

'Well, I think you had better bring him. When a man gets to such an age the heart may fail at any moment—you would feel easier if you had the doctor.'

'I'll go for Dr. Morton now,' said Pat, 'I hope he will be at home.'

Dr. Morton was in his house and came back with Pat. He talked to old Michael and examined his heart, but it seemed much as usual—he could find nothing really wrong with him, nothing that would account for the old man's belief that he was about to die almost at once.

'Come—what makes you think your time has come now?' he asked him.

'I just know it, doctor. They called me last night.'

'They? Who?'

'Who but me old comrades—the men I drilled with and marched with back in '67—before any of ye were born? I'm the only wan left of them all now—and my time has come at last.'

Old Conroy was evidently getting senile, thought Dr. Morton. Well, as he had said, it was time for him to go, and he hoped, for the sake of the young people, that he would not linger on in that state for very long. A fine type, of course, and no doubt a grand man in his day, but it was nearly time for him to depart this life. Ninety-two years of age—a great age—too long for any man. The doctor, tired after a long day's work, feeling a bit off colour himself just then, hoped that he would not live so long. An old age, existing on the pension of a dispensary doctor in Ireland, would not be very pleasant.

'Well, goodnight, Michael,' he said. 'Try and sleep and you will feel better in the morning.'

'*Goodbye*, doctor,' was the quiet reply, and Michael held out a hand, veined and wrinkled. The doctor shook it with a smile—as one who humoured a child. Downstairs Pat and Margaret were waiting for him.

'Well, doctor—what do you think of him?'

'He seems much as usual, except for this obsession that he is going to die tonight. I have seen cases of this sort before, and strange to say, they generally did die. I don't know whether it was auto-suggestion or what—but the fact remains that they died when they decided to do so! But with regard to your grandfather—it would be impossible to say how he is, Pat. I must be off now and try and get some sleep before Mrs. Doyle at the Cross sends for me as she is likely to do tonight, and I think it is twins this time!'

When the doctor had gone, Teresa went upstairs to sit with the old man. He was in a doze when she entered the room, and she sat looking at the old face on the pillow, wondering what it must be like to live so long. To live to be over ninety. What a changed world it was from the one which he could remember when a boy. What would the world be like in another ninety years? What would Science have done for the good—or destruction—of mankind? Teresa had no thoughts of another World War. In that year 1936 the world was apparently at peace.

The old man had suddenly opened his eyes.

'So ye are there,' he said, 'I'm glad. I have not long to live now and I wanted to talk with someone who can talk to me of Ireland—someone who loves the land.'

'But we all love it—Pat and Margaret, too,' replied Teresa.

'Not as we love it. Young people these days are different, they don't remember the time when we had to fight for our country—no, nor the names of those who died for Dark Rosaleen. Ask any school child ye like for the names of those men who were shot by the English in Easter Week, and could they tell ye? No—they could not for I have asked them many a time. Talk to me now about that week in Dublin—for ye were there and can remember it all.'

She told him—as she had often done before—all she could remember, and then they spoke of him who they both had loved—the dear lover of her girlhood.

'Ah, yes—they were good men and true—those of Easter Week,' said Michael Conroy, 'but I knew as good long before ye were born. Girl dear—but ye should have known those of the Fenian Brotherhood! A hard fight they had—and they were defeated and scattered, but they sowed the seed. What was it that Pearse said at the grave of O'Donovan Rossa?'

Teresa recited for him the closing words of Pearse's oration at the great Fenian's funeral, and he repeated softly after her: 'Our Fenian dead—aye, they have left us our Fenian dead! The fools—the fools!' And from those dead sprang the Easter Rising.

'You can remember the Fenian Rising?' asked Teresa. She had often heard him speak of that far-off time, but knew he loved to tell of it.

'Aye—I mind it well. Wasn't I with them—a young man, not much more than a boy I was then. But I joined up, drilled with them, marched with them, our hopes and our heads carried high. Well, it came to nothing—we were defeated, some of us arrested and sent beyond the seas. Many's the time I wish I had been with those who suffered for Ireland's sake—banished from their own land, as the "Wild Geese" and others had been before them—sent into exile by those who had no right in this country at all. Aye—it's bitter to think of!'

'But it's all over now, Michael,' said Teresa, 'the British have gone. We have our country ourselves now.'

'The British gone, is it? What about the Six Counties of Ulster where they are still masters? And look how they are trying to anglicise us down here by their books and newspapers—the cinema and radio? We are not free as long as one inch of Irish soil remains in British hands. We are not even Irish yet—and I doubt if we ever will be!'

'Oh, don't take that view!' said Teresa, 'I'm sure that the Six Counties will be ours some day and perhaps before very long. And as for the books and papers, and so on, well no one country can remain isolated these days.'

'I don't want us to be isolated, but I want us to be Irish—so really Irish that foreigners will know what we are—and not mistake us for English people.'

Teresa could say nothing. She remembered a holiday she had once taken abroad, and of how she had always been taken for an English woman until she announced her Irish nationality. Even then, in one shop, the owner had said, in puzzled and rather contemptuous tones: 'But you speak the same tongue—is it not so? How, then, is one to know the difference?'

But old Michael was getting tired—strangely tired. She noticed the change in him, he grew sleepy, his talk wandering. It was now past midnight and Margaret and Pat were sitting up with her. It was getting chilly and Margaret made up the fire, blowing the turf so that it blazed cheerily in the open grate. They had some tea and then sat quietly, only speaking in low tones now and then, for the old man seemed to be sleeping. But in his sleep he would mutter to himself, and at times was very restless and uneasy. Presently he sat up suddenly in bed, as if listening to something. 'They are coming,' he said then, 'don't ye hear them? They thought he was wandering until they, too, heard a sound from without—a loud sound like the tramp of men marching. They listened in amazement. What could it be? What men could be marching there, in that quiet spot at this hour of night? Nearer and nearer came the tramp of feet. They looked at one another, those three who heard, but some strange fear kept them from looking to see what it was.

Then Pat rose to his feet and went to the window. It was moonlight without, and he could see the garden path and the gate and the road beyond. It lay there plain to be seen in the light of the moon. Nearer and nearer sounded the feet—they were passing the very gate it seemed. Yet nothing and no one could be seen. The road was empty.

But the old man on the bed raised his head and smiled.

'They are here,' he said, 'they have come for me—they have not forgotten.'

And then as the marching feet went on past the gate, down the road, he sat up in bed and cried in a loud voice: 'Glory O!—Glory O! to the bold Fenian men! I am coming to join you—old friends!' the hand was raised in salute, 'God save Ireland!' cried the old Fenian—and fell back on the pillow.

Michael Conroy had gone to join the host of the Fenian Dead.

CHAPTER XVII

A NEW VENTURE

'Yes, there are six children, but the two eldest attend school— the Kindergarten up the road. You would not have much to do with them—just to keep their clothes in order, see to their baths, and their meals which they will have with you in the nursery. You would have entire care of the other four. Baby is just a year old, Cecil is three, Clare four, and Dorothy six. George and Violet, the two eldest, are twins—they are a little over seven. So you see what a fine family I have! You will be required to see to all the wardrobes, to keep their clothes in good repair, and so on. I hope you are a good darner?'

'Yes, I think so.'

'I am glad of that. They wear out their stockings and socks so quickly. I shall expect you also to wash baby's things and help with the washing of the others. Now do you think you can undertake that work and do it efficiently?'

Nora was silent for a moment. She had not thought that the work would be so hard—that she would be expected to do all these things.

As she did not speak, Mrs. Dempsey looked at her sharply. This woman, the wife of a rich publican, whose barmaid she had been before he married her, believed in getting her money's worth from all those in her employment.

'Perhaps you do not feel strong enough for the place,' she said, 'and if I were to engage you I should certainly expect you to be quite capable of performing your duties in a satisfactory manner. I give good wages—thirty pounds a year, all found—but you will, of course, provide your dresses and aprons. You will have an evening off once a week when either cook or the housemaid will take your place in the nursery. You also have a half-day off each month— which I consider quite good.'

Still Nora did not speak. She was wondering if she would ever be able to look after all these children, see to their clothes, do the baby's washing, take them out—be with them practically all day. She had not been used to such work—office work with its regular hours was so different. It was only as a last resource that she had thought of a situation like this.

A New Venture

'Would you allow me to consider it for a little?' she asked. Adding: 'I could let you know my decision tomorrow,'

'Well, really, it is not usual to allow maids to keep a mistress waiting while they consider whether they will take a situation or not—it is generally the other way round. However, you seem a quiet, decent girl, and I think would suit if you feel strong enough, so I agree to wait until tomorrow. But please call as early as you can.'

Mrs. Dempsey was really making a virtue of necessity. She would not have agreed to wait for Nora to consider the matter but for the fact that she had had very few applicants for the situation of nursemaid to her young hopefuls. They were all spoilt, pampered children, and there had been a succession of nursemaids during the last few months. The place was a hard one, the pay poor, according to present-day standards, the time-off bad, too. Nora looked so ladylike, was so quiet, so well-mannered, that Mrs. Dempsey felt here indeed was the girl for whom she had been looking. She seemed one whom it should be easy to keep in proper subjection. Very presentable, too. Mrs. Curran, next door, would wonder where she had got such a superior person and would probably think that she was one of those trained children's nurses. A vulgar, ostentatious woman, Mrs. Dempsey liked to impress her neighbours.

Nora went back to Whitechurch feeling very downhearted. Mrs. Dempsey had been the only person who seemed inclined to engage her. There others told her frankly that she looked delicate and was not the kind of nursemaid for whom they were looking. The truth was that Nora's appearance was rather a puzzle to these ladies who wanted a good strong girl to look after their children. Not only did Nora seem rather delicate, but also she was decidedly not of the class to which they had been accustomed when engaging their maids. There really might be something fishy about her— one never knew these days! So, after a morning of disappointments, Nora had been glad when she saw that Mrs. Dempsey seemed inclined to engage her, but when she heard the number of children and all she would be expected to do, the girl could but doubt whether she would be able for the work. If her health broke down again, what would she do?

She talked it all over with her friends that evening. Mrs. Gilfoyle and her daughters were strongly opposed to her taking such a post, but their opposition only served to strengthen her resolve to make the effort. She felt that she must be independent—that she could no longer remain under such obligations to these good people who had been so kind to her. She must try and earn her own living—someway—somehow.

'I have made up my mind to try it,' she said. 'After all it may not be so hard as it seems.'

So the following morning she returned to Mrs. Dempsey and told her that she would take the situation. That lady was gracious in a pompous sort of way.

'Very well, Nora,' she said. 'I am glad you have made up your mind, and I am sure you will like the place—the children are such little dears. And now when can you come?'

'Whenever it will suit you, madam.' Nora had decided to address Mrs. Dempsey in this manner instead of the usual 'Ma'am,' which seemed to stick in her throat, and Mrs. Dempsey, who knew that Nora's mode of address was used by the domestic staff of big houses, was quite pleased.

'Well, let us see, this is Tuesday—we will say Thursday. Be here about tea time so that the children will all be here. By the way, I hope you have a good stock of frocks and aprons—and of course caps.'

'That will be all right, madam.'

Mrs. Gilfoyle was providing her with what was needful, and Nora had insisted that she pay her back from her first month's wages. Mrs. Gilfoyle had tried to prevail upon the girl to accept such a small gift, but Nora would not hear of this. Even at this moment, while she was having her interview with Mrs. Dempsey, her good friend was waiting for her at the bus stop just outside the gate of 'Mount Alverno', the big, modern, hideous house on the Rathfarnham road, where the Dempseys lived. Mrs. Gilfoyle, looking at it, thought that it must be like its mistress—it was so vulgar and glaring, one of these new monstrosities which are doing their best to destroy the old-world beauty of Rathfarnham. She also thought to herself that if Mrs. Dempsey was as vulgar as her house, then she and Nora would hardly agree. And Mrs. Gilfoyle would not be sorry if this business came to an abrupt end. She thought it absurd and ridiculous altogether that a girl like Nora should try to undertake such work—she was totally unfitted for it. But she knew the girl's pride and respected her for it. She must let her try this place for a short time, and pray that something better might soon turn up.

A New Venture

When Nora appeared, she said little to her, and they proceeded into town, where Mrs. Gilfoyle bought such things as she considered absolutely necessary for this mad scheme.

That evening Nora went to see Teresa and tell her about her new work. Teresa was surprised, and, like Mrs. Gilfoyle, did not approve of it at all, nor did she think that Nora would stay very long with Mrs. Dempsey. But she said nothing to discourage her, it would be best to let the girl take her own way. She knew that Nora wanted to be independent, no matter how hard she might have to work.

Besides, Teresa had had some news that morning which was worrying her a good deal—for she did not know whether she should tell Nora about it or not. She had received a letter from Margaret Conroy—such a happy letter—breathing in every line a happiness which Margaret herself seemed hardly able to believe could be true.

'You will be surprised when I tell you that Harold and myself are going to be married,' she wrote. 'You know, of course, that he was engaged to Nora Tiernan. But I don't know whether you are aware that she is the daughter of John Tiernan, the man who robbed Harold's father and caused his death? She deceived him and his people, and Harold could not forgive her conduct. I do not want to be hard on her now when I am so happy myself, but I do think she treated him in a terrible manner. I can only hope that I may be able to make up to him for a little of all he had suffered.'

Teresa had known all the sad story, Nora having confided in her, feeling that she could do no less when Teresa had been so good to her. Never could she forget that frightful Christmas Eve and Teresa's kindness then. So that part of Margaret's letter was no news to Teresa. But that Harold was going to marry her—that was news indeed, and for Teresa it made sorry reading. She had known Harold only slightly, having met him but a few times when she was on visit to Cross Roads Farm. But she had liked what she had seen of him. And she had not thought that he was the kind of man to change so quickly from one girl to another. 'I suppose his mother influenced him,' she thought, 'or maybe he has just agreed to marry Margaret in a spirit of indifference—not caring much what he does. Well, I am sorry. I had always the hope at the back of my mind that he and Nora might yet come together and forget all that past tragedy. I never thought that Harold was so hard.'

Nora was telling her all about Mrs. Dempsey, asking her advice on the proper management of children, and so on, but Teresa was hardly listening, her whole mind concentrated on the one question: 'Shall I tell her or not? Ought I to do so?'

Nora noticed her abstraction at last. 'What is it, Teresa?' she asked. 'What are you thinking about?'

Then Teresa made up her mind, she would tell her. Better that Nora hear it now from a friend than that some outsider should blurt it out, when she was unprepared.

'I heard from Wexford today, Nora,' she said.

She had already told Nora of her friendship with the Conroys, but she had not mentioned to her that Margaret and Harold had been friends for years. But Nora knew of the friendship, she sometimes remembered how jealous she had felt of Margaret when she had met her, recognising the sterling qualities of the girl, her unselfishness, her innate goodness of heart. She had sometimes wondered, too, how Harold could have preferred herself. But lately, since all that was over, she had thought but little of Margaret, any reason she had had for jealously was gone. Her feelings seemed dead, all that had passed between her and Harold was as a dream that had faded, never to return—to be forgotten for always if that were possible.

Yet her feelings were not so dead as she had thought them to be. They awoke with a sharp stab of pain as Teresa went on: 'Margaret had some news to tell me—rather unexpected news, too.' She paused a moment, and instinctively Nora knew that this news—whatever it might be—had some connection with Harold. She waited quietly for Teresa to proceed.

'Margaret is to be married,' she said, 'married to Harold Hastings.'

She did not look at Nora while she spoke. She could imagine the pain in the dark eyes, the look of anguish on the pale face.

There was silence for a moment, and then Nora said, quietly: 'Thank you for telling me, Teresa.'

She said nothing further, and Teresa saw that she did not wish to discuss the matter. They had tea together and talked of indifferent subjects; of Mrs. Doyle and her foolishness over the idle George; of Mrs. Pat who was expecting her seventh baby; of little Miss Moran, whose dog was just now attending the vet to have some of his teeth extracted, and of her anxiety about him. Even

A New Venture

when Nora was saying goodbye she did not mention the Wexford news, only speaking of her new venture.

'Goodbye,' she said, 'I will come and see you when I get my evening off. Of course I must see them at Lilac Tree House first—they will be anxious to know how I am getting on.'

'And so will I,' said Teresa. 'Good luck now—and remember what I told you about the children. Don't spoil them, let them know that they must be obedient.'

'I am afraid that will mostly depend upon Mrs. Dempsey,' said Nora.

'Oh, you must stand up to her—those kind of women need taking down a peg or two.'

Easier said than done, thought Nora, as the bus took her back to Lilac Tree House. When she went to bed that night—wondering when she would sleep there again—she tried not to think about Harold and Margaret. But, needless to say, she could not help thinking of them—seeing them together, thinking of him speaking to Margaret as he had once spoken to her—the dear, tender voice. She wondered would he tell Margaret that he was a 'grand hand at making tea,' like he had done on that night which now seemed a hundred years ago. And his beloved face—she prayed that she might never see him again.

'Dear God,' she whispered, 'This is my penance, I accept it as such, but don't ask me to ever meet him again—never let me see him!'

On the following day she set off for her new situation. Molly Byrne, the housemaid, admitted her. 'The mistress is out,' she told Nora, 'but she told me to show you your room and the nursery, and then you are to get ready to have tea with the children.'

Molly was rather puzzled by the appearance of the new nurse-maid; she herself was a good-natured, country girl, but she thought that Nora looked more like a lady coming to call than as one of the maids.

Nora was to sleep in a room off the nursery, where there was also a cot for the baby. He was a fat, chubby child with a perpetual smile, and Nora took to him at once. For the others she did not care much, especially for the two eldest, George and Violet, the twins, who treated her in a very careless manner—it was evident that they had learned from their mother to treat servants thus.

The work was hard, and Nora soon found that she never had a moment to call her own. She had to wash and dress the younger ones in the morning, and call the elder ones and see they had their breakfast and were got off in good time for school. She had to wash up after the nursery meals and keep it and her own room clean and tidy. The children—including the baby in a pram—were taken for a walk before their mid-day dinner; in the afternoons she helped the elder ones to prepare their home lessons—not that they had many to do—and if fine, there was another walk before tea. After tea the children were bathed and got ready for bed, and then she had to do any washing or mending which might be required. She had hoped that she would have a few moments to herself in the evenings but soon found her mistake—there was always some kind of work to be done. The darning alone took hours. She went to bed sometimes too tired to sleep. On her first evening off she would have liked to go straight to bed, but knew that was impossible, for Molly, who was taking her place, would be coming in to put baby to bed, so she pulled herself together, changed into her own clothes, and set off for Lilac Tree House.

When her friends saw her they exclaimed at her appearance.

'My dear girl,' said Mrs. Gilfoyle, 'you will never be able to stay at that place! I knew it was not fit work for you. Why not give notice at once and come back to us?'

'No—I will stick it out,' replied Nora; 'after all, I have a roof over my head, and food to eat—oh, yes, I know how gladly you would have me back again—you are so good—' her voice broke, but after a moment she went on: 'Still I would rather stay with Mrs. Dempsey for a little longer and see how I get on. I will be more used to the work after a while.'

And she stayed. Mrs. Dempsey was quite gracious to her, in her usual rather pompous manner. She liked Nora's appearance, her manner with the children, the baby had taken to her, but above all, several ladies of her acquaintance had made enquiries as to where she had got such a superior nursemaid for her children.

'I suppose you are giving her very high wages?' asked one, and without telling an absolute untruth, Mrs. Dempsey managed to convey to their minds that she was doing so. 'But then, you know,' she said, 'that she is a very superior young person.'

And then, suddenly, without warning, there came an end to all this.

On one of Mrs. Dempsey's 'At Home' days, Molly happened to be ill with a bad bilious attack. 'Eating far too much—that's all that's wrong with that one!' said the cook. Mrs. Dempsey sent the children to play in the garden, where the baby was asleep in the pram, and she told Nora that she would require her to help in the drawing-room with the tea. So Nora carried in the tea and helped to hand round cakes and sandwiches to the assembled ladies.

'Have you called on Mrs. Dillon yet?' asked one of them.

'Yes, I called last week,' said Mrs. Dempsey, 'and I expect she will be here today.'

'She made a good match for a girl in her position—didn't she?' remarked one of those present in an undertone to the lady beside her.

'Yes, indeed,' was the reply, 'and she is not really good-looking—too much make-up and all that, and not even in her first youth.'

'Hush—here she comes!' warned the other.

There was a general turning of heads towards the door as the newly-married lady was seen to enter. She was a tall, showily-dressed woman, with a shrill, unpleasant voice which reminded Nora of someone, but she could not remember who it was. She could not see the lady very well, the others were crowding round her with their congratulations, and she was laughing, seeming to be in very good humour.

'Nora—bring some fresh tea for Mrs. Dillon,' called Mrs. Dempsey, and Nora went to bring it.

'Haven't them ones finished swilling down tea yet?' asked the cook as she make a fresh potful.

'I declare to God I never seen their like!'

On her return to the drawing-room, Nora poured out a cup and brought it with cream and sugar to Mrs. Dillon. It was then that she nearly dropped all upon the carpet. In the person of Mrs. Dillon she recognised Rose Malone—a very grand and glorified Rose—but herself all the same. And if Nora was surprised, so was Rose. However, she said nothing at the moment, and continued her conversation with the lady beside her. But she stayed rather late, remaining after the others had all gone. And it was then that she spoke to Mrs. Dempsey.

'May I ask,' she said, 'if you won't think it impertinent of me, 'what is the name of your parlourmaid?'

'Oh, that is really my nursemaid—the housemaid is, unfortunately, not well today, so I had to ask Nora to take her place.'

'Nora?'

'Yes—Nora Tiernan—a most superior girl, is she not?'

'And you feel quite satisfied with her?'

'Oh, yes—she is quite a treasure, so nice mannered and so efficient with the children.'

'And you have not—missed anything since she had been with you?'

Mrs. Dempsey stared at her guest. 'What do you mean?—I don't understand.'

'Well, it's not my business, of course,' replied Mrs. Dillon, in dulcet tones—quite reluctant, seemingly, to speak—'but I happen to know all about this girl, and I could not recommend her to anyone. Certainly I would not allow her near children.'

'You must please tell me what you mean,' said Mrs. Dempsey. 'Nora Tiernan had not been long with me, but while she has been here I have had no fault to find with her, and as to her honesty—I think you must be mistaken, Mrs. Dillon.'

'I do not think so. I knew this girl when she worked in the same office as myself. I was the bookkeeper, she was one of the typists. She then called herself Nora Malcolm.'

Mrs. Dempsey gave a gasp. 'But why did she do that?'

'Because she would find it hard it get work if people knew who her father had been.'

She then told Mrs. Dempsey the story of poor John Tiernan, adding in sorrowful tones: 'I'm sorry to say that I think she must have inherited some of her father's bad characteristics—she resembles him in that I have reason to believe she is not honest. While she was at Murphy's we girls in the office missed quite a number of things—one girl her fountain pen, another her scarf, I lost a good pair of gloves myself. But the climax came when one of the girls lost her purse with her week's salary in it. I then thought it my duty, being the senior of the office staff, to acquaint Mr. Murphy with the facts which had come to my knowledge some time before. A friend of mine happening to see Nora Tiernan in the office had told me the truth about her. I had not liked to make the matter public or harm the poor girl—I am not that sort. But now I felt I must do my duty, however unpleasant it might be. So I spoke to Mr. Murphy. He sent for the girl and she admitted all. She left the office that day and I have not seen her since until today.'

A New Venture

Rose paused, she wished to make a good impression on Mrs. Dempsey, but at the same time she wanted to do all the harm she could to Nora without this being suspected by her hostess. So she added, in kindly tones: 'But, of course, dear Mrs. Dempsey, if you think you can now trust the girl, then let her stay by all means. But I should not put temptation in her way—keep as much as you can under lock and key.'

Mrs. Dempsey was thunderstruck, she could hardly believe all this.

'Are you *quite* sure, Mrs. Dillon, that this is the same girl? I can hardly credit it.'

'Perfectly sure, but if you are in any doubt, why not ask the girl herself? Have her in here now—it will be the best thing to do.'

'Yes—I will do so,' replied the other, 'for I cannot but think that there is some mistake.'

Nora heard the drawing-room bell and guessed at once what it meant. It was her duty, anyway, to answer it this evening when she was doing duty for Molly.

When she entered the room both Mrs. Dillon and Mrs. Dempsey turned to look at her. She made a pretty picture, standing there in her neat blue frock and frilly apron. What a pity it would be if she had to let this girl go, thought Mrs. Dempsey, such a superior person, quite an asset to the staff at Mount Alverno. Surely Mrs. Dillon must be mistaken. Well, she would soon find out.

'Nora,' she said, 'this lady says she knows you. Is that so?'

'Yes, Madam.'

'Where did you meet her?'

'She was bookkeeper in Mr. Murphy's office when I was there, too.'

'What name did you go under then?' suddenly asked Rose.

'I gave my name as Nora Malcolm.'

'But why?' asked Mrs. Dempsey.

'I had my own reasons for doing so.'

'And did you have to leave on account of various articles being stolen from the office?' went on Rose.

'I left after an interview with Mr. Murphy—but I did not steal anything.' Nora lifted her head proudly as she spoke and looked Rose full in the face. That lady laughed.

'So *you* say!' she replied.

Mrs. Dempsey was terribly vexed and put out. So it was true—this girl had deceived her. Of course she might have known that there was something queer about her. She was altogether too 'grand' for her present situation. She could not possibly keep her now—all her friends would hear about this, she was sure that Mrs. Dillon, in spite of her would-be kind manner, was a gossip, and a rather malicious one too. Her acquaintances, who had envied her such a superior maid, would now have the laugh at her. She felt perfectly furious with Nora.

'I am afraid I shall have to ask you to leave,' she said, 'but you will be paid a month's wages in lieu of notice, and by doing so, I consider that I am treating you very well—better than you deserve.'

'Very generous, indeed,' murmured Rose.

'Thank you, madam,' replied Nora, 'but I will leave at once and not trouble you for any wages.'

Mrs. Dempsey looked uneasy. Nora did not look like a guilty person, perhaps there was some mistake after all. Yet the girl had not denied the truth of what Mrs. Dillon had said.

Rose was speaking again. 'I think, Mrs. Dempsey, if you don't mind me saying so, that you would do well to have this girl's boxes searched before letting her leave the house.'

Nora's face flamed. She saw red for the moment and could have struck Rose Dillon in her fury. But reason and self-control reasserted themselves and came to her aid. She would take this insult with the cold contempt which it merited. It was not the first time she had had to leave in disgrace—she thought of that morning in Mr. Murphy's office. But that had not been quite so humiliating—she had not received such an insult before leaving.

'If you wish to search my things please come upstairs, and do so at once,' she said to Mrs. Dempsey, quietly ignoring the other woman as if she had not been present. 'I wish to leave your house without unnecessary delay.'

Feeling rather small, in spite of the support of Rose Dillon who went with her, Mrs. Dempsey went upstairs to Nora's room and searched it thoroughly, also the suitcase, which was all the luggage she had brought with her. Finding nothing, they went back to the drawing-room, from the window of which Rose soon had the satisfaction of seeing Nora go down the garden path on her way to the bus. Thus she was once more dismissed from her post through no fault of her own.

CHAPTER XVIII

THE WHEEL OF FORTUNE TURNS

'Well, I am very glad you left that place—but as for Rose Dillon—words fail me!' Thus said Mary Gilfoyle when she sat listening to Nora's story on her return from the office that evening.

'Did you tell me that she was married?' asked Nora.

'Yes, indeed I did! Don't you remember? she married that old Mr. Dillon who used to buy all the seeds for his garden from Murphy's. He is a rich man, and has a fine place near Rathfarnham—mad on gardening. Rose had a grand wedding, I believe, but of course none of us were invited—not swanky enough!'

'What a cat that woman must be!' said Anne.

'Well, there is no need for you to worry about the matter at all,' said Mrs. Gilfoyle, 'no one who knew you would ever believe that you stole a pin from anyone. And I am very glad, as I said before, that you have left that place—it was not the right kind of work for you.'

'But what am I to do now? Oh, I know that you would not mind how long I stayed here, but don't you understand that I must be independent?—I must earn my own living!'

'Yes, I quite understand how you feel, and we will talk about it in a day or two when you are rested and have got over this unpleasant experience.'

Mrs. Gilfoyle would not let her talk any more about the matter, and Nora was glad enough of the peace and quiet at Lilac Tree House. But at night when she went to bed, it was long before she could sleep, thinking of all her troubles, wondering if she would be able to get something to do. It seemed so hard, she was able and willing to work, yet was prevented from doing so on account of what her father had done. It was not fair—surely there must be plenty of other people whose fathers had been far worse men than her poor daddy, and yet they could get work—and were allowed to keep it and to work in peace. There seemed to be some fatality over her. In spite of the kindness of her friends—kindness which she knew to be real—Nora felt desolate indeed that night. And, as always when she was depressed her thoughts went back to Harold and her love for him. She wondered would he be happy with Margaret—would she be able to make up to him for all he had suffered in the past? Did he really love her as he had once loved another?

Nora Tiernan felt desolate and alone, deprived of her lover, prevented from earning her living—cast alone upon the waves of the world. Why was it, she wondered? Surely she had done her penance. Had she not suffered enough for her wicked deception? Many a one sinned more deeply, yet did not suffer so much as the result of their sins. 'At least not in this world,' whispered a voice to her soul, 'but what abut the next?' Yes, she thought, what about the next—better to suffer here than afterwards. Perhaps God in His Mercy was giving her that chance to make reparation now instead of in the hereafter. A little comforted, she fell asleep just as the birds were beginning to sing their matins in the trees outside her window.

Mrs. Gilfoyle insisted that she rest for a whole week after her strenuous time with Mrs. Dempsey. She felt better in every way at the end of that time, and on Monday morning began again her endless search for work. Her friends advised her to try again for office work, but as Nora would not pretend that she had not been previously employed, and could not produce a reference from her former employer—the result was always the same, she was not suitable. Nora herself would have taken any kind of work, no matter how hard and distasteful—she would have gone as waitress in a fish and chip place, as assistant to a small shop-keeper, even as messenger girl—anything at all by which she could make her living. But Mrs. Gilfoyle was determined that she would not allow this. Nora was growing more unhappy and depressed day by day as time went on, it seemed so unfair when she was willing to work—and work hard at anything.

The days passed and autumn had come. The trees were decked in many-coloured splendour, the apples and pears ripe, the hens laying less eggs. 'Winter will soon be here,' said Anne one day, 'how I wish it were always summer!' A wish which Nora echoed from the bottom of her heart. She had grown to dread the winter, its cold and wet, when her coat was thin and her shoes bad. One thing she had put her face resolutely against—she would not allow Mrs. Gilfoyle to buy her clothes. And to this resolve she held tight.

One morning a letter arrived for her with the address of a well-known firm of solicitors on the envelope. Her hands shook as she opened it. Was it possible that here at last was a chance of employment? She had inserted an advertisement in several of the papers,

The Wheel of Fortune Turns

in a desperate hope that something might come of it. Was this an answer? But she supposed it would be just to ask her to call for the usual interview which would end in the usual way. Mary was setting off for the office but waited a moment to hear what news Nora might have—she so hoped that it might contain a chance of work.

She watched Nora opening the envelope and reading the letter, but she had barely read the first lines when she gave a little cry; she seemed unable to speak, she could only gaze stupidly at the letter in her hand, as if she were not capable of grasping its meaning.

'What is it, Nora?' asked Mary. 'Have you got a job at last?'

Still without speaking, Nora pushed the letter across the table to Mrs. Gilfoyle. These were the words which had so surprised Nora:

> 'Dear Madam,
>
> We have to inform you that your paternal aunt, the late Mrs. Amelia Dolan, died recently in Melbourne, and by her Will you inherit her entire estate. As this is very considerable, we should be glad if you would be so good as to call at our office at your earliest convenience, when we shall have the pleasure of going into all necessary details with you.
>
> Hoping that we may have the favour of acting for you in the settlement of this matter,
>
> > We are, etc., etc.'

Mrs. Gilfoyle looked at Nora with a smile. The girl was still sitting as if stunned—too dazed to speak.

'Why, Nora, my dear, I am so glad! It seems that your hard times are over at last.'

Nora nodded. 'Yes—I suppose so,' she agreed. 'It seems so strange, I hardly know anything about my Aunt Amelia, except that she went to Australia when a young girl and married out there. She seldom wrote to daddy, and before his—death, had not done so for some time. I do not know whether she—whether she knew—about him.'

'Well, that is no matter now,' said Mary, while Anne cried: 'Oh, hurry—and you will just catch the bus and be early at Mr. Roper's office. I am dying to know all about your fortune!'

A short while later, Nora sat in the private office of Mr. Charles Roper, the senior partner of Messrs. Roper, Carey and Roper, solicitors, and listened while he gave her more details.

It appeared that her aunt, Mrs. Amelia Dolan, had been a wealthy widow, whose husband had died some years previously, leaving her in complete control of his fortune. There were no children, and apparently Mr. Dolan had no near relatives. Anyhow, Mrs. Dolan had made her Will, leaving everything to the daughter of her brother, John Tiernan. It seemed by this Will that Mrs. Dolan had known of the death of her brother. She had probably seen the account of the tragedy in some Irish paper. The money left was a very large sum, and when death duties and other expenses had been paid, Nora would inherit approximately the sum of forty thousand pounds. Messrs. Roper had agents in Australia, and it so happened that it was one of these Australian solicitors who had acted for Mrs. Dolan when she made her Will, so that Mr. Roper had been communicated with at once.

Nora was almost dazed. How strange—incredible—it seemed to her that after her hard time with Mrs. Dempsey which had ended in such an ignominious way—that now she was a rich and independent woman, and could figuratively snap her fingers at them all. Mr. Roper, a fatherly old man with daughters of his own, glanced at her shabby coat and worn shoes.

'If you would allow us to make you a small advance until this business is finished, we should be most happy.'

Then as she did not reply, he said that the settling-up of affairs might take a little time—some weeks—and therefore she might as well have some money to go on with—there might be arrangements she would want to make?

Nora hesitated a moment or two, but the thought of her friends at Lilac Tree House and their kindness to her decided her to accept Mr. Roper's offer. Now she need no longer be a burden on those who had been so good to her. She would take the money and bring them home a little present. Perhaps a rich cake for tea. That Mr. Roper would offer her more than a few pounds never crossed her mind. But that gentleman, seeing not only a pretty girl whom he was glad to help, but also a wealthy future client, pulled out his cheque book.

'Well, how much shall we say? A hundred—two hundred—five if you like.'

'Oh, a hundred will be plenty,' said Nora. Adding: 'But are you sure it will be all right? That you will be able to repay yourself?'

Mr. Roper laughed as he made out the cheque. 'I only wish you every happiness with your good fortune. Oh, by the way, I had better give the bank a ring to let them know it is all right to pay you. That is if you have not an account yourself.'

Nora smiled ruefully. A bank account—and she with not a penny but what the Gilfoyles gave her.

'No, indeed,' she said, 'I have no bank account anywhere.'

'Ah, well, that will soon be all changed,' said Mr. Roper. He put his message through to his bank and then shook hands warmly with Nora. 'You may expect to hear from us shortly when we have further particulars from Melbourne. Goodbye now—and take care of yourself!'

He accompanied her himself to the door of the public office—a distinction only shown to important clients.

Nora made her way to the bank, and stared in wonder at the cashier who could ask: 'How will you take it?' in the same indifferent tones as it he were remarking that it was a fine day.

With the hundred pounds in her purse, Nora was out in the street once more. What should she buy? What a lot she could get now. She could have gone into any shop and have bought herself a new coat and frock, new shoes, underwear—everything of which she stood so badly in need. How often lately she had gazed wistfully at the shop windows thinking of all she would buy—if only she had the money.

Yet now, so excited was she that she could not stay for any shopping until she had told her news to them all at Lilac Tree House. But she must celebrate a little—they must have a little spree! So she bought cakes and sweets, cold ham, meat pies, fruit and other tasty things for a high tea that evening. It was so delightful to have money to spend as she liked—and to know that there was plenty more to come—when she had been through such terribly lean times for months now.

There followed days of delightful shopping. Nora bought presents for them all, and for herself clothes and other articles which she so badly needed.

She was called for several interviews with Mr. Roper about her affairs. How different, she sometimes thought, were these interviews with this solicitor from those other ones when she had been a humble applicant for work. Now she was an important client ushered in and out of the office with due deference. At last all was settled, death duties and other expenses paid, and Nora found herself possessed of the sum of forty-five thousand pounds. It seemed stupendous to the girl, and she listened without much interest to the various projects put forward by Mr. Roper as being good investments. There was only one thing upon which her heart was set. She was resolved to buy a house, if possible in the neighbourhood of Lilac Tree House. She had always wished for such a place, and after a few weeks of searching the advertisements, going to house agents and auctions, she at last found the very house she wanted. It was but a mile from Lilac Tree House, a fine old Georgian building of grey stone. The gardens were large and in good condition, the former owner having only left it a short time. Behind the house could be seen the Dublin mountains in all their loveliness, while from the front of the house the city lay beneath, with the well-known landmarks plain to be seen, and in the distance, on a clear day, the Irish sea might be discerned. It was a delightful spot, even on the rather dull day in early December when Nora and Mrs. Gilfoyle first saw it. It had a beauty and charm all its own and Nora was delighted that at last she had found what she wanted.

'But what a big house just for yourself!' cried Anne, one day when she and Mary had gone out to see it with Nora.

'But it is not all for myself,' she replied. 'I intend it to be a place where anyone I know or hear about who is in want of a rest can come and stay for a while—the workers of the world—the old or the delicate. I will make it a place to which they will be glad to come, summer or winter. Girls like myself, who are city typists, would surely like a real rest with good food, nothing to pay, and allowed to do just as they like all day. And those who are out of work, would it not be a blessing to them? I know what it is to be poor and to be looking for a job—day after day, day after day, to be worrying how to pay my rent, how to buy food and clothes. I can never forget those days last December, just a year ago, before dear Teresa came to my help—and then you—how lonely and desolate I felt. So I want to be able to help anyone who finds herself—as I did—up against it. I have had this plan in my mind ever since I knew that this money was mine.'

'That would be grand,' cried Mary. 'You could start with Teresa—she could come there for her holidays.'

Nora smiled. 'Teresa is coming for all time,' she said, 'she has promised to come and take charge of the place for me. She understands those kind of things better than I do. I am so glad she is coming and I had hard work to persuade her, but at last I got her to consent. She will act as a kind of Matron when our guests arrive and when the house is full, her work will not be too easy—she will earn her salary all right!'

A busy time followed, the house was in need of papering and painting, and there were also some repairs to be done. A gardener and a boy to help him had to be got and the servants engaged. Amongst those who applied was Molly Byrne, former housemaid at Mrs. Dempsey's. Her surprise at seeing Nora coming calmly to interview her was ludicrous, and Nora was greatly amused at seeing Molly. She had always liked the girl, who, in many ways, had been kind to her during that terrible time at Mount Alverno, and to Molly's huge delight, she engaged her. A good cook and parlourmaid completed her staff of domestics. Later on Nora might require more help if her visitors were numerous. Grey Manor, as the house was called, could accommodate a good number.

The weather was damp and cold. Rain came instead of frost, cold rain which seemed to penetrate to one's very bones.

One evening while Nora was going through the gardens with the new gardener, explaining some alterations she wished done, she caught a chill. She did not notice how cold she felt until she was cycling back to Lilac Tree House. When she reached there, her teeth were chattering with cold, and she was shaking all over. Mrs. Gilfoyle put her to bed at once and gave her hot milk, plenty of blankets, hot water bags to her feet, a big fire in her room. But in spite of all, Nora shook and shivered. In the morning she was very ill with a high temperature, and Mrs. Gilfoyle sent for the doctor. He was soon able to diagnose pneumonia. Teresa came to stay in the house and there were also two nurses. Nothing that could help to bring her over the crisis safely was left undone. Every modern treatment was tried, but Nora did not seem to respond as she should have done.

'It is as if she had no wish—no will—to live,' remarked the doctor in puzzled tones to Mrs. Gilfoyle.

That lady knew what was the matter with Nora, why she had no great wish to live. In her delirium the girl had again and again called aloud the name of 'Harold'.

Never since she had told Mrs. Gilfoyle the whole truth of her engagement to Harold had Nora again mentioned his name. Only now, when self-control had vanished from the sick mind, when her thoughts had gone back to scenes which now seemed like nightmare dreams, when her woman's heart once more longed for the man whom she loved so dearly—only now did Nora breathe his name again.

She grew weaker, and it seemed as if she knew herself how weak she was. There came a morning, just before Christmas, when she received the Last Sacraments. She lay quiet and calm for some time afterwards, but so weak that she could hardly move her hands.

'Is there anything you would like—anything you want to say?' asked Mrs. Gilfoyle, 'if so, tell me, dear, and I will do my best to help you.'

The girl did not speak for a moment. Then she raised her eyes—so shadowed and sunken now—to Mrs. Gilfoyle's kind face.

'I would like to see Harold,' she said, 'just to say goodbye to him—only to say goodbye. And he might—he might forgive me now.'

CHAPTER XIX

THE MESSAGE

Margaret Conroy was walking homewards to Cross Roads Farm from Mrs. Hastings' cottage where she had been spending the evening, and Harold was with her. It was just ten o'clock on a fine frosty night, the stars shining overhead, their feet ringing out sharply on the frozen ground. The weather had changed during the last few days, and from being damp and wet, had turned to a bright, dry frost—seasonable weather for the time of year, people said, for it wanted but a few days to Christmas. Holidays had already commenced and Harold had come to spend his with his mother and aunt—and near the girl to whom he was engaged.

Margaret's face, beneath her little fur cap, was glowing with happiness—such happiness as it had never worn before. Always happy in a quiet way, calm, serene, going about her work, both in the house and out of doors, with a cheerfulness which sometimes she had found it hard to maintain, yet never before had she felt the radiant happiness which now filled her whole being. Radiant, there was no other word which would express it. Yet, so great was her happiness that, at times, she felt almost afraid. That Harold, whom she had loved so dearly for years, and whom she had schooled herself to think of as another's lover, that he should have turned to her in his trouble and asked her to be his wife—this seemed too good to be real. Was it but a fairy dream from which she would soon awaken and come back to the old grey life of duty and self-denial? And then she would pinch herself and be glad to feel the pain which told her that she had not been dreaming. His people were so glad, too. Mrs. Hastings who had felt deeply the deception which Nora Tiernan had practised upon her, was now plainly delighted that Harold was going to forget the girl who had treated him so badly, and was about to marry one whom both she and her sister knew and trusted so thoroughly. Harold had spoken but little to Margaret about Nora. He had just said that he had made a mistake, and was trying to forget it now—and would Margaret help him to do so? How gladly she had promised and how eager she was to be of any help to him. What would she not have suffered to bring ease and a little happiness to him?

They had been engaged now for some months and were to be married at Easter of the coming year. His mother had wished the wedding to be sooner and had mentioned the New Year, but Harold, remembering another marriage with another bride which was to have taken place in the early days of the present year, held to his resolve that this wedding should be at Easter. And Margaret was only too glad to do as he wished in this as in all other matters.

When they reached the farm Harold went in with her for a few minutes. Pat was sitting by the big turf fire in the kitchen and looked up at them with a grin as they entered.

'Hello—you pair of turtle doves!' he said, with a grin, 'so here you are. Cold, isn't it?'

'Freezing,' replied Harold.

'But I like it at this time of year,' said Margaret.

'I hope it keeps this way for Christmas. You are home early, Pat.'

'Yes, Eileen had a cold and didn't want to go to the pictures, so her mother asked me in and I stayed with them for a while and then came home.'

Eileen Casey was the girl to whom Pat Conroy was engaged and whom he was bringing as mistress of Cross Roads Farm when Margaret had married and left him. Glancing at her and Harold now, Pat found himself thinking that they were not very lover-like to one another—so quiet and undemonstrative. He and Eileen were not so polite—almost cold—to one another. Thinking of Margaret's marriage, Pat was sorry that she was going away to Dublin. It was not far, of course, but it would be city life, and what could a girl like Meg, used to life on a farm, do in the city? How would she adapt herself to it? Harold was taking a flat near Merrion Square, a nice enough place for those who could fancy such a life, but it wouldn't be Pat's fancy—and somehow he did not think it was Meg's either. But if Harold was cool and apparently not too deeply in love, Meg was different. That she almost idolised Harold was obvious. Pat knew that she had loved him for years, although so well did she hide her feelings that her brother was probably the only one who had guessed her secret. The only one, that is, with the exception of her great-grandfather. The old man had been almost uncanny in the way he could see through people—read their very thoughts. A queer old man; and although he and Pat had not always got on well together, and the younger had rebelled again and again against the other's old-fashioned ways, still now that Michael had gone, Pat found himself often looking rather wistfully at the corner seat beside the fire where the old man had sat, every night, expounding his views on the world in general, railing at modern fashions, bemoaning the lost days of his youth. Pat often remembered, too, the night when Michael Conroy had died—the queer sound of tramping feet going past the house—down the road and yet nothing to be seen. Imagination? Perhaps. Yet they had all heard those marching feet, and certainly Teresa Mason was not one to imagine things. And then those words of the dying man—he too had heard those feet. Well, Pat supposed that the real meaning of it all would never be known. It was just one of those queer things which one came up against now and then.

Harold got up soon to go and Margaret went with him to the gate. They did not linger over their goodnights after the usual manner of lovers. Harold kissed her gravely, quietly, as a brother or old friend might have done. Margaret stood at the gate for a few moments, looking after him as he swung down the road with never a backward glace. Suddenly her eyes filled with tears, her lips moved in prayer. A great fear had descended upon her—she felt as if she were watching him go from her for ever.

'Dear God!' she whispered, 'leave him to me, please! Let us be happy together.'

Harold's thoughts were very different. It was more than a year since he had seen Nora, since he had learnt the truth about her and had written her the letter which had parted them for ever. Yet of late, his thought had persistently turned towards her—far more so than they had done at first, when the heat of his passion blinded him to all else but her wilful deception. But now it was different. All through the day, he found himself thinking of her, remembering her face, the expression of her eyes as they were raised to his, all the pretty ways she had—so gentle, so kindly. Who could have believed that she could have deceived him—lied to his mother—and probably laughed at their gullibility. That was the most bitter thought of all—Nora deceiving him—laughing at him. Could she have done so? could she—who had seemed to care so dearly for him—could she have really rejoiced in the deception—been amused at the easy way she had led them astray? But the lies she had told! Her father a commercial traveller, dying of pneumonia—and all the time he had been John Tiernan, the dishonest suicide—the man who had robbed his father of thousands of pounds and been the cause of his death. Harold was not naturally a hard or vindictive man, but he had loved his father dearly—they had been more like brothers than father and son, for James Hastings had had a lovable, boyish nature. His financial ruin—through no fault of his own—and his death which had followed so quickly, had made an indelible impression upon his son, and Harold, watching the grief of his mother, seeing the poverty to which she was reduced, had vowed that if ever he could be revenged upon the relatives of John Tiernan, he would take that revenge. Mrs. Tiernan had died soon after her husband, but a daughter remained. Harold had never seen her, and he sometimes wondered what she would be like—the daughter of such a man as John Tiernan. He happened to hear casually from a solicitor friend that she was trying to obtain work as a typist. This man had refused to employ her, and both he and Harold advised several people against her. Then she seemed to have vanished completely for he heard no more about her, and he concluded that she had left the country. That she was still in Dublin and had obtained work under another name never entered his head. And then they had met, and not knowing who she really was, he had loved her from the very first moment that he saw her—loved her with all the love of his heart, and had thought that she loved him too. But she could not have done so, because if so she would surely never have deceived him so brazenly. Well, he had done with her now—parted from her for ever. But now he wished that he could *forget* her. He could not get her out of his mind, her lovely face, her ways—the way she talked, the way she had of smiling with her eyes. Oh, but he could have sworn that she was good and true, sincere. And yet——

He had hoped that his engagement to Margaret would have helped him.

It had not done so—rather had it accentuated the difference between the two girls. He knew Margaret to be all that he had once thought of Nora—truthful, sincere, to be trusted in every way—a girl whom any man might be proud and happy to call his wife. Then why could he not be at peace and forget that other? Why must he think of her by day—dream of her by night? And those dreams were the worst of all. Only last night he had dreamt that he was standing on the slopes of Tibradden mountain, on the

The Message

very spot where they had been on that day when he had asked Nora to marry him. He went towards her, but no matter how quickly he seemed to walk, he never got any nearer to Nora. He knew, however, that she was doing her utmost to reach his side—to speak to him. He tried to put from him all remembrance of this strange dream as he reached home and entered the room where he found his mother sitting alone by the fire.

'Why, Mums—not in bed yet?'

'I am just going, dear. You look tired—are you not well?'

'I'm all right.'

'You left Margaret at home? Did you see her brother?'

'Yes, he was there. Eileen had a cold so he was home early as they did not go anywhere. Now, Mums—off you go to bed.'

But Mrs. Hastings lingered a moment. 'Dear Margaret looked very well this evening—don't you think so?' she remarked.

'Yes—very well.'

'You cannot think Harold, what a joy it is to myself and your aunt to know that you are making her your wife. It was a terrible disappointment to us when you were thinking of marrying the other.'

'Please say no more about that, mother. It is over and done with. Now go to bed, like a good lady, and sleep well.'

'You will be going soon yourself?'

'Yes, quite soon.'

But for some time after his mother had left him, Harold sat by the embers of the turf fire, thinking—remembering. And when he went to bed at last he was visited again by the same dream—the hillside near Tibradden and Nora standing in the distance with outstretched hands, trying to reach his side.

He awoke, feeling tired and unrefreshed. His mother and aunt were already at breakfast when he got downstairs, and Harold sat down to his with little appetite. He had just finished and was thinking of going for a good tramp to put himself into better form, when he saw the telegraph boy getting off his bicycle at the gate.

'Why, here is a telegram,' cried his aunt. 'I do hope it is not for you, Harold, to call you back for some tiresome legal business.'

'Oh—no, I don't expect anything of that sort,' he replied. Yet it was with a strange feeling of fear and misgiving that he took the wire from the boy. It was addressed to him, and he opened it, standing there in the pretty living-room, his aunt clearing away the breakfast things, his mother watching him anxiously. Just at first the words danced before his eyes, making little sense, then after a moment he found himself reading them over and over, repeating them to himself. He was not surprised, hardly unprepared. After all, had he not been really expecting something like this—almost waiting for it?

'Nora dangerously ill. Asks constantly for you. Teresa.'

Without knowing it, he dropped the message to the floor as he turned towards the door. His mother picked it up and read what was written. Hardly could she believe her eyes. Teresa Mason sending him a message—and from that girl! 'Harold,' she called quickly, 'where are you going?'

'To Dublin.'

'But—but surely you are not going to see—*her*?'

'She may be dying—I am going to her.'

She ran after him, grasped his arm. 'Harold! You cannot mean it? You are not going to her?'

He shook off her hand, being for the first time in his life almost rude to his mother.

'She may be dying—or dead!' was all he said.

He left the room, and in a few moments she saw him striding down the road to catch the Dublin bus.

CHAPTER XX

RENUNCIATION

'I could not love thee, Dear, so much,
Loved I not Honour more.'

'I wonder will he come?'

The speaker was Teresa Mason, and she and Mrs. Gilfoyle were sitting in the warm kitchen of Lilac Tree House. Outside the snow was falling thickly, turning the Dublin mountains into snow-covered sentinels, guarding their beloved city which lay, like a picture, beneath them.

The house was quiet; in the sick-room Nora was dozing fitfully after a restless night; in another room the night nurse was asleep, taking her well-earned rest, and Nurse Cullen, the day nurse, was sewing by the fire in Nora's room.

This case was puzzling Nurse Cullen—as well it might. Who ever heard of a pneumonia who had passed her crisis and come successfully through it, and who yet refused to gain strength and get well? And that although everything that money could buy and loving care could think of surrounded her; all that medical science could supply, the newest treatment for pneumonia—all was at her disposal. Pneumonia cases are not, nowadays, regarded as being very serious when the patient is young and healthy, and Nora, if not particularly strong just then was yet healthy and had youth on her side. By every known rule she should now be gaining strength daily, yet far from doing so, she lay there, listless and weary, having seemingly no interest in life, no desire to get well. Nurse Cullen, puzzled over it all as she sat by the fire and watched the snow falling from the grey skies. Other points about this case puzzled both herself and the other nurse. It was evident that there was no lack of money. Anything that doctor or nurse suggested was got at once—every attention was shown to the sick girl. The two nurses sometimes talked over the case together.

'They cannot be wealthy people,' said Nurse Dempsey, 'the house is so small, and one of the daughters and the mother do the housework, and the other girl works in an office in town—yet money seems plentiful, nothing is ever wanting—look at the expensive dainties they buy to try and make her eat.'

'Yes, and they do us well, too,' said Nurse Cullen; 'they are jolly decent every way.'

'But what is wrong with the girl that she won't try and get well?' asked the night nurse. 'I wonder is there a boy friend in the story?'

'Well, there is no sign of him,' replied Nurse Cullen; 'no letters, no inquiries.'

'I was thinking they might have had a quarrel,' said the other, 'and maybe that is what is keeping her back.'

'Well, perhaps. There is certainly something on her mind, but I don't think it is a love affair,' replied Nurse Cullen, who, unlike her colleague, was not romantically inclined.

Yet at that very moment when she was thinking of what Nurse Dempsey had said, and pondering idly as to whether there could be any truth in it, and while downstairs Teresa was saying to Mrs. Gilfoyle, 'I wonder will he come?' Harold was reading the telegram which Mary had dispatched on her way to business that morning.

He arrived at Lilac Tree House that afternoon. Teresa was with Nora, Nurse Cullen being off duty. Nora, as usual, was lying there quietly, listening to all that Teresa said and speaking when necessary, but evidently taking no interest in anything. It had stopped snowing, but there was that queer stillness in the air which comes with the snow, and all sounds seemed muffled. But Teresa's quick ear heard a car stop at the gate and then a ring at the door. Glancing at Nora she saw the sick girl had half risen in her bed and was looking towards the door of the room with flushed cheeks. A moment later Mrs. Gilfoyle had entered, and standing on the threshold was Harold Hastings. There was a little cry, 'Harold!' from the bed, and as he strode froward, Mrs. Gilfoyle beckoned to Teresa and they both left the room.

Harold had not spoken, he had reached the bed in a couple of strides and gathered the frail little figure into his arms. At that moment he completely forgot that she was the daughter of the man who had robbed his father—the girl who had deceived and lied to him. Looking at her now, lying there, so helpless, so pale and wan, he only saw the girl whom he loved. With an inarticulate cry he held her fast in his arms as if he could never let her go again. And there was silence for a space, neither of them speaking.

Then Nora said: 'So you came—you forgive me?'

'There is nothing to forgive,' he replied, almost fiercely. And in truth all his anger, all his bitterness were swept away, blotted out as

Renunciation

if they had never been. This girl, looking at him with such a world of entreaty in her deep-shadowed eyes, was the little Nora who had crept into his heart the very first time they had met on the slopes of Bray Head—all else was forgotten. Forgotten, too, were other things; his engagement to Margaret Conroy; his mother and aunt and what they would say. Nothing mattered, nothing was of any importance in the whole world except the one fact that he loved Nora and that she was once again in his arms.

But her next words shattered his brief dream of joy.

'Oh, Harold—I am so glad you forgive me! I did so want to hear you say so before I died.'

He stared at her speechlessly, the words of the telegram coming back to to him—words forgotten in the momentary joy of reunion.

'What are you saying?' he asked.

'But you know—don't you—that I am not going to live? That is why I wanted to see you so much—just to beg your forgiveness, although I know I do not deserve it. Mrs. Gilfoyle told me this morning that she had sent for you, but I did not know if you would come. Oh, Harold—I loved you so much! I could not bear that you should know about my father's disgrace. And then when I knew who you were—heard it all from your mother—then I think I went mad. I just seemed to care for nothing, not to mind what lies I told—how I deceived you. But it was all because I loved you so—I felt as if I could not let you go. And yet I had to after all—you see how I have been punished.'

'But you knew my name from the beginning,' said Harold in puzzled tones.

'Yes, but I had never been told the name of the man whom my father had wronged. My mother said before her death that it was better I should not know it. But you see she was wrong.'

'I wonder,' said Harold. Then he said: 'But you are not going to die. Nora, my little love, you must live for me—promise me that you will. Now that we have come together again we must never part. We will forgive and forget. Our love will wipe out all old debts between us, and we will write "Paid in full" to them all. We will start afresh. Nora, you must not talk of dying—you are so young and surely you wish to live—for my sake.'

She was silent a moment, looking at him in mute surprise.

'But we can never be anything to one another now,' she said then.

'Why not?'

'Have you forgotten?'

'Forgotten what?'

'Margaret.'

'*Margaret!*' With lips gone suddenly dry he could hardly form the word. Yet a second later he repeated: 'Margaret! My God! I had forgotten her.'

'But I had not. If I had not remembered her I would not have agreed to let them send for you. It was because I knew that you were engaged to her and so could not think that I—that I was trying to make things be as they were before. Ah, no, Harold! I just wanted to hear you say that you forgive me—and then I can die in peace.'

'But it must not be!' he cried. 'I will explain to Margaret—tell her everything. She will surely understand—will see reason. She is a decent sort, and would not wish to stand in our way.'

'And don't you think that I am a decent sort, too? From what you have known of me in the past, you may not have reason to think so. But at least I am decent enough to refuse to allow you to treat Margaret like that. Harold—my dear—you must keep your word to her—you must marry her.'

'I cannot—I cannot!'

'You must. My darling—don't you understand that I wish to make up a little for the way I acted in the past. You must help me to play fair. We must be honourable—both of us. You must keep your promise to Margaret—and I must give you up to her. It may atone a little for the way I have acted.'

He did not speak for a few moments. His heart was dead within him, desolation of soul swept over him. Had he found Nora only to lose her again for ever? How could he marry this other woman now? A woman to whom he had been perfectly indifferent—whose very existence he had forgotten when face to face once more with the girl he really loved. Yet somewhere within him a tiny voice was speaking, telling him that there was something higher and nobler than all else. And that was Honour. Honour for which men and women have gladly died.

He leant forward, resting his face on her thin hand as it lay on the coverlet.

'I will do what you say,' he murmured, 'but, my darling, it will be hard—and you must help me.'

Renunciation

Nora suddenly remembered one evening when she had toasted muffins for tea, and had sat waiting for him. Instead he had sent a letter, and she had known then the very bitterness of death. But she did not remind him of it, she only said, 'We must help each other and God will surely help us both.'

They talked then, a long, intimate talk, such as those who have been separated by misunderstanding will have together. Nora told him everything, her temptations and sufferings, hiding nothing from him; her hopeless search for work, telling him even of that terrible Christmas Eve, which had brought to her aid such real friends as the Gilfoyles and Teresa Mason. But one thing she did not tell him—and that was the change in her own fortunes. She had very special reasons for not telling him about that.

As Harold listened to her voice he felt a terrible remorse—a remorse made all the worse by the knowledge that he could never make up to her now in any way for his treatment of her—never give her the happiness which she so deserved. As for the fact that she was the daughter of the man who had robbed his father and been the cause, indirectly, of his death, that seemed to matter nothing now—to be of but little importance. He loved Nora and she loved him. That seemed to wipe away all the past. If it were not for Margaret—but there was no use thinking about that now.

They had been talking for over an hour, but to them it seemed but a few moments, and they were surprised when Teresa entered, carrying a tea tray.

'Now, Nora, here is your tea,' she said, 'toasted muffins as you asked; and I have brought a cup for the visitor.'

She smiled at Harold as she spoke, but glanced keenly at him as she put down the tray. What was the result of this interview between the two, she wondered?

Nora was smiling at Harold also. 'Muffins for you,' she said, 'I know you like them. Will you pour out for me, Harold? You told me once that your were a grand hand at making tea—do you remember—so I am sure you can pour out nicely.'

But Harold rose quickly to his feet. 'Don't ask me, Nora,' he said. 'I could not do it. Let me go now—it is better so!'

Taking her in his arms, heedless of Teresa standing there in bewilderment, he kissed her once—a kiss of renunciation—and then putting her gently back on the pillows, stumbled from the room like one gone suddenly blind.

Teresa stared after him for a moment, hearing his step in the hall, then the front door opened and shut, the next moment the gate clanged and there was the sound of a car going swiftly down the hilly road.

'Well, that's that!' said Teresa, and turned towards Nora. 'If he won't take any tea—you may as well have yours—you must want it.'

But as she went to the bedside she saw that the sick girl had fainted.

CHAPTER XXI

TERESA TAKES A HAND

Nurse Cullen was very angry when she returned from her walk to find the patient, whom she had left all right, now much weaker, only recovering from a bad fainting fit. She spoke about it to Nurse Dempsey when she went, as was her custom, to the pretty parlour where the night nurse was having her meal. There the two nurses gave each other their reports about the patient, and so were left alone to talk.

'She seemed quite all right when I went off duty at three o'clock,' she said. 'I only went as far as Rathfarnham for a walk—it had stopped snowing and I wanted a breath of air. Then when I came back there was Mrs. Gilfoyle in a panic and the girl looking like death.'

'What about Miss Mason?'

'Oh, she was quite cool, of course. Had done all that was necessary. But how she—a trained nurse—could have allowed visitors who were likely to upset her——'

'Visitors! But she was not to have any!'

'Well, they let her have *one*, anyway, this afternoon. He was not long gone when I came back on duty.'

'*He?*'

'Yes, a male! And I think I passed him on the road near here, in his car. I begin to think, Dempsey, that there may be something in your boy friend idea.'

'But they should not have let her see him so soon.'

'That's right. But, on the other hand, they may have thought that if they did not do so now, it might be too late. Dempsey—do you really think that girl is going to die?'

'No—at least up to this I never thought so. But this upset may be pretty bad for her.'

'Yes—and that's why I was so mad with them—doing a thing like that on their own, without asking us. Of course, Mrs. Gilfoyle knows no better, but I am surprised at Teresa Mason.'

Teresa was vexed with herself, too, when she saw the bad result of Harold's visit. She had been against it when Mrs. Gilfoyle told her how anxious Nora was to see him. 'She wants to ask his forgiveness,' she said, 'it is an obsession with her, and I believe it is keeping her from getting stronger. I feel sure that if she could see and talk with him—found that he did not harbour any ill-feelings against her—she would grow easier in mind and stronger in body.'

'It might upset her too much—better to wait a little,' Teresa had replied at first. But eventually the older woman had persuaded her to let Mary wire to Harold, and it had been done—and this was the result. Nora was decidedly worse—the meeting with Harold had done her harm and not good. Teresa blessed Mrs. Gilfoyle for a meddlesome old fool, yet she was just enough to blame herself, more, for she, with her training and experience, should have known better. Well—it was done now, and she could only hope and pray for the best, and be more careful in the future.

As to Nora herself, she had been so glad to see him—to learn from his own lips that he forgave her—that just at first she had felt better—almost well again. But the pain of giving him up, of seeing him go from her when she could have had his love for her own for evermore—this had been too much for her. With his goodbye kiss her strength seemed to go from her and a great darkness descended upon her which she thought must be death itself.

But when she regained consciousness she knew that she was still alive—still upon this earth. Thoughts of the man she loved—a great longing for him—came upon her so vividly that nothing else seemed to matter. She lay there quietly through the long hours of the night, making no demands upon the attention of Nurse Dempsey, asking for nothing, swallowing her medicine and any drink when they were brought to her. She was too quiet altogether for the night nurse who would have preferred to see her more troublesome. Several times she asked her if there was nothing she would like, nothing which she could get for her? Always the reply was the same, Nora wanted nothing and was quite comfortable. But if her body was quiet, her mind was not, and the night nurse had to report that the patient had not slept at all during the night.

Yet Nora felt that she should not have anything to worry about. When the doctor had taken a grave view of her case, the priest had come and administered the Last Sacraments, and that same day Nora had sent for Mr. Roper and made her Will. She had explained to him just what she wanted done and he had put it down with all due legal formalities. In plain words Nora had made provision for the upkeep of Grey Manor, including a good salary to Teresa, who was to live there and oversee everything. She then told Mr. Roper that she wished to make restitution—as far as money could do so—to Mrs. Hastings. For this end she set aside the sum which she believed to have been the amount taken by her father, with one thousand pounds in addition. She had two reasons for making the additional sum: first, because she felt it to be only right that something over and above the exact sum should be paid, and secondly, she did not wish that Mrs. Hastings should have any clue as to who had sent the money.

'It is to be sent to her at once,' she told the lawyer, 'as an anonymous gift. You can make it all right—can't you? Say it is from an old friend, or something like that. But I want it arranged at once—whether I die or not.'

'You are not going to die just yet, my dear,' replied Mr. Roper. 'I find that when people make their Wills they very often take another lease of life.'

The residue of her fortune Nora left to Mrs. Gilfoyle and her daughters, not forgetting a legacy to Teresa.

So on this morning—just four days before Christmas—as Nora lay there so quietly, trying to realise that Harold had gone from her for ever—that she would in all probability never see him again, she also tried to keep her mind from dwelling too much upon such things but to rather concentrate on spiritual things and the state of her immortal soul. She was feeling so terribly weak that morning that she had little hope of recovery. And, after all, what incentive had she to make her wish to get well? None. Her future spread itself before her, dull, grey, like the winter dawn. She wished it were a summer's morn when the dawn would come early, ushered in with the song of the waking birds. She thought of some mornings in summer when she had lain awake in that same room, worried and anxious, wondering if she would soon get work, and remembered the little bird which would begin to sing before any of the others—a lovely, tender little song. She did not know what bird he was, but had pictured him as a little brown bird, sitting on a branch by himself and singing his early matins in thanksgiving for the dawning day. After him would come the sparrows in the ivy outside the window. A different note was theirs—all chatter and fuss and quarrelling.

But on this cold winter morning—so near to Christmas—there were no birds singing, although at breakfast time Nurse Cullen would spread crumbs on the window sill and they would fly down and take them. The cold had made them bold, and there was a robin who even came into the room. These thoughts mingled with others in her tired brain, so that she could hardly rouse herself when Nurse Cullen came to sponge her and make the bed.

'She seems pretty low this morning,' said the nurse to Teresa as she stood talking for a few moments in the kitchen. 'She is so listless and has no desire to get better, as far as I can see.'

Teresa only murmured something, she had affairs of her own to attend to that morning. Nurse Cullen thought her almost callous, considering that she was so much to blame for Nora set-back.

When the doctor called he was extremely annoyed to hear from the nurse about Harold's visit. He interviewed poor Mrs. Gilfoyle downstairs.

'I distinctly said that no visitors were to be allowed—perfect rest and quietness were essential in her present weak state. I must ask you to obey my orders in the future. The solicitor was necessary, of course, as you informed me she had some money matters to settle, but besides him and Father Dunne, no one else was to be allowed to see her. Whoever the visitor was yesterday, she is certainly the worse for seeing him. Had Nurse Cullen not been off duty, she would have seen that no one was allowed in the sick room. If you cannot assure me that my orders will be obeyed, I shall be compelled to call in a third nurse which will mean needless expense and should not be required—especially as you have Miss Mason here. I am indeed surprised that she should not have been more careful, and I should like a word with her.'

But it seemed that Miss Mason was not in the house. She had gone to visit some friends living at a distance, and it was uncertain when she would be back at Lilac Tree House.

Teresa had had but little more sleep than Nora, and in the weary watches of that night she make up her mind to a definite plan of action.

So, on the evening of that same day she was seated with Margaret Conroy in the cosy living-room of Cross Roads Farm. She had had a wearisome, cold journey, the bus being overcrowded at that time of year, and she was glad of the bright fire and the substantial tea which Margaret had hastened to set before her. But Teresa did not seem hungry, and Margaret looked curiously at her now and then, wondering what brought her down to the farm at such a time and so unexpectedly. Teresa sat there after tea, warming herself and talking to Judy, who seemed delighted to see her again. Since the death of Michael Conroy the old dog had appeared to lose heart, she was always looking for her old master always expecting to hear his voice—to feel his hand resting on her head as they sat together by the fire. No one else could take his place with Judy. She suffered the attentions of the others with grave politeness, but showed them plainly that it was her master for whom she waited. She was glad to see Teresa—it seemed as if she regarded her as a link with the old man, and she showed her pleasure in no uncertain manner.

'I suppose she misses her master?' said Teresa.

'Yes, very much. Poor old dog—I am afraid she is breaking up. She has fretted so much.'

'And how are you keeping yourself—and Pat?'

'Well'—with a smile—'you can see that I am all right, and Pat is grand, getting all sorts of improvements done to the farm.'

'When is he to be married?'

'At Easter.' She smiled again and coloured as she added: 'We have arranged to have the two weddings on the same day.'

How happy she looked, thought Teresa, and as she watched that happy face and sparkling eyes, and thought of the object of her visit, her heart almost failed her. But there was another who surely deserved her pity more.

'I suppose you see Harold every day,' she said, 'now that he is home for the holidays?'

'Yes, he comes most days, but I did not see him yesterday—he had to go to Dublin. I expect he will call some time tonight.'

'Yes—I know he was in Dublin.'

'You know?'

'Yes. He came to Lilac Tree House where I am staying with the Gilfoyles.'

'He had business with them? Or did he go to see you?' asked Margaret, with a happy smile.

'No—not to see me or the Gilfoyles either.' She paused a moment and then went on: 'He came to see Nora Tiernan.'

'*Nora Tiernan?*' Margaret stared at her in bewilderment. She wondered if Teresa were jesting. Still she would hardly jest on such a subject.

'Yes, to see Nora. She is very ill. She has had pneumonia, and although she got over her crisis all right, she seems to have no wish—no desire—to live. And I think that is the reason why she is not getting strong.'

Margaret stared at her, hardly at first comprehending her meaning. After a moment she spoke. 'I am sorry,' she said, and added coldly: 'I hope she will recover.'

'She was very distressed by Harold's visit,' said Teresa.

'No doubt. I suppose she wished him to forgive her for her lies and deception—no wonder she was upset when she remembered how she acted.'

Teresa did not speak for a moment. 'He gave her his full forgiveness,' she said then.

Margaret said nothing more, and when she spoke again it was to make some remarks about the farm. But Teresa felt that she could not sit there quietly any longer—she must speak—must say what she had in her mind. Her journey must not prove useless.

'Margaret!' she cried, 'I came here to tell you about them and you must listen to me. They love one another, and are both breaking their hearts. Yet in honour Harold feels bound to you. But all his love is given to Nora as hers is to him. Oh, if you could only see them you would understand! And you would be sorry for her—I know you would! I firmly believe that if they could come together again, Nora would soon regain her health. If not—she will die.'

'Am I responsible for that?'

'You can give him his freedom.'

'Why am I to give up the man I love—the man I have loved for years—long before he ever knew of such a person as this Nora Tiernan? And look at how she behaved to him—her lies and deceit!'

'I know—I know! But, Margaret, it was all for love of him—she completely lost her head—and she has been sorry for it ever since.'

'Yes—when she knew her lies were found out!'

'Oh, Margaret—don't be hard! If you love Harold now is the time to prove it.'

'You know I love him. I love him too much to let him ruin his life by marrying that girl.'

Teresa was silent. It seemed hopeless to try and soften the heart of this girl. Never before had she seen Margaret in such a mood—she who was always so kindly to all, so gentle to man and beast, there was not an animal on the farm which did not know and love

Teresa Takes a Hand

her. But here, indeed, was a different Margaret—hard and cold. It would be useless to talk to her further—anyway at the moment. Perhaps in the morning——

But the disappointment was great. Teresa had had such hopes of being able to talk Margaret round—to persuade her to do a noble thing—to sacrifice her own feelings for the sake of the man she loved. And she had found a Margaret she did not know.

She rose wearily from her chair. 'I am tired,' she said, and she did feel suddenly very tired, 'I think I will go to bed. I know it is very early, but if you don't mind, I'll go now.'

'Very well,' replied Margaret, 'I have put you in the spare room.'

She went upstairs with Teresa, saw to it that the fire was burning brightly, the hot water bag in the bed. She was the perfect hostess if somewhat cold.

'Would you care for some hot milk or anything else?' she asked.

'No, thank you.'

'Then I will leave you to rest. You must be tired. I hope you will sleep well. Goodnight.'

'Goodnight,' replied Teresa.

CHAPTER XXII

A CHRISTMAS GIFT FOR NORA

Tired as she was, still Teresa could not sleep for some hours. It was early and she had so much to worry her. She heard Harold arrive, and a good while afterwards Pat came home. Then, in a short time, all was quiet, Harold left and the others went to bed. Tired out, Teresa fell at last into a deep sleep.

Some time in the night she was suddenly awakened by some sound. At first she was so stupid with sleep that she could hardly rouse herself to full consciousness, yet she knew that the same sound was going on, over and over again. Then at last she was fully awake, and realised that it was someone sobbing. Bitter sobbing. Margaret's room was just across the landing from where she was, Pat slept further away. Teresa got out of bed and cautiously opened her door. Yes—it was as she had thought—the sobbing came from Margaret's room. She went across the landing and knocked softly at the door. At once the sobs ceased. Teresa waited a moment and then knocked again. Rather loud and regular breathing could now be heard, just as if Margaret were fast asleep. But Teresa knew better. She opened the door gently, and in a whisper said, 'Margaret!' There was no response except the same deep breathing. Margaret evidently did not want her to know that she was awake, perhaps she hoped that her sobs were not heard. Teresa went back to her room and all was quiet until the morning.

She did not sleep very well afterwards and was downstairs early as she wanted to get back to Dublin as soon as possible. She had no wish to stay longer at the farm. Her mission had failed—the sooner she left now, the better.

Delia brought her breakfast, and when Teresa asked for Margaret the woman said she was feeding her hens. But before she had quite finished Margaret entered and Teresa's keen eyes saw at once that the girl had had a bad night, she looked wretched, pale and haggard. Teresa wondered why this should be so. Had her conscience pricked her for speaking so harshly about Nora? However, she said nothing about what she had heard in the night and Margaret kept her own counsel. Indeed there was little time for talk as Teresa was catching an early bus. Margaret was coldly polite—nothing more. Both felt the tension, and it was a relief when it was time for Teresa to go. The goodbyes on both sides were cold and restrained. But at the last moment, moved by some sudden impulse, Teresa turned at the gate and called back to the other: 'Happy Christmas, Margaret!' She saw a queer spasm pass over Margaret's face as if from some great pain, and then she replied, quietly: 'The same to you!'

Then she turned back to the house, Judy at her heels, and Teresa sped down the road to meet the bus.

During the homeward journey, she could not help thinking about Margaret—wondering how she could have changed so much. Even if she were determined not to give Harold his freedom, at least she might have replied in a different way. Teresa had known her for many years—they had been such friends. She had always thought so highly of Margaret—so serene and calm, so patient with the old man when he had been in one of his bad moods. She was loved by everyone, those in trouble came to her for help—for sympathy. The well-known lines—'A heart at leisure from itself to soothe and sympathise' had always seemed suitable to Margaret. She had seemed so unselfish—perhaps selfless would be the better word. And now she had found her hard and cold—a very stone.

Mrs. Gilfoyle and Anne were not so surprised as Teresa had been. They had not known Margaret, and naturally thought that she would not be inclined to give up the man she loved. Indeed Mrs. Gilfoyle had thought it a harebrained notion and had been surprised that the sensible Teresa should ever have thought of such a thing.

Of course nothing had been said to Nora, she thought that Teresa had gone to stay the night with friends in town. She was glad to see her back, and smiled a welcome when she came as usual to sit with her while Nurse Cullen took her time off.

Mrs. Gilfoyle was busy in the kitchen, Anne having gone to Rathfarnham, when a ring came to the door. Opening it she was amazed and angry to see Harold Hastings.

He was smiling as he held out his hand but received no smile in return.

'What do you want?' asked the lady.

'To see Nora, of course! How is she?'

'She is not well at all. Your visit greatly upset her and did a lot of harm, she had been much worse since. No!'—as he took a step forward—'you cannot see her—the doctor left strict orders that you were not to do so.'

'But I must see her! Listen, Mrs. Gilfoyle, I am engaged to Margaret no longer and I want to tell Nora.'

'Come in,' she said, 'you must explain more fully.'

He followed her into the pleasant sitting-room, and when they were both seated, she said: 'Now tell me just what you mean.'

'I mean that Margaret told me last night that she did not intend to marry me. She gave no definite reason, and when I asked for one only said that I could tell Teresa Mason that she was sending me as a Christmas gift to Nora.'

Mrs. Gilfoyle stared at him. 'So that explains it,' she exclaimed.

'Explains what? What do you mean?'

'Teresa went to see Margaret yesterday and told her how ill Nora was. She begged Margaret to release you from your engagement to her, saying that she thought Nora would die otherwise, as at present she had no wish or desire to live.'

'And Margaret agreed?'

'Far from it. She absolutely refused, and Teresa returned terribly disappointed.'

Harold was silent for a moment, staring at her.

'I wonder what made her change her mind?' he said then, 'I am puzzled.'

'I am not,' replied Mrs. Gilfoyle, 'the answer is—love. That girl loves you so much that she could make even that sacrifice for your sake.'

'You mean——'

'I mean that she has given you up so that you can marry Nora, because she knows that you love her. Teresa's journey was not in vain.'

But Harold had sprung to his feet. 'I may see her now?'

'No, I don't think so. I would be afraid, it might upset her too much, the shock would be so bad for her. Besides, the doctor gave strict orders——'

'Oh, dash the doctor! Come, Mrs. Gilfoyle! Be a dear and let me see her. It will do her good—you'll see it will!'

And so rather against her will she let herself be persuaded, and with visions of an enraged medico before her eyes, took Harold upstairs and knocked at Nora's door.

Teresa opened it, and at sight of Harold uttered an exclamation of dismay and was going to shut the door behind her while she spoke to him. But to her astonishment he grasped both her hands

A Christmas Gift for Nora 149

and shook them while he said: 'God bless you, Teresa! I will never forget what you did for me!'

Then before she could speak, he had entered the room himself and shut the door upon her and Mrs. Gilfoyle.

Nora had her face turned away from the door and she thought it was Teresa who entered.

'Who was that knocking at the door?' she asked.

There was no reply, and turning her head she saw who it was.

'Harold!' she gasped. 'You should not be here!'

'Yes, I should. My place is at your side always from now on.'

It took him a little time to explain, for Nora was almost too dazed by his news to comprehend it fully at first. But presently the meaning became clear to her. She lay there with his arms around her wondering if it could really be true. No—indeed she must get well. Now she must live for him. She felt the urge to live—to get strong and well. How happy she was—how happy! How good God was to her after her lies and wickedness.

And then she remembered one who by reason of her great happiness must be unhappy indeed.

'Dear Margaret!' she said. 'I am so sorry for her. Oh, Harold, how good she is!'

'Yes, she is,' he replied. Then added, with masculine blindness: 'But don't worry, darling, I don't think she really minds much. She seemed quite casual—just said that she had been thinking things over and had come to the conclusion that we were not suited to each other.'

He said nothing about Teresa's visit to Wexford, he thought it better not to mention that to her. Nora was silent for a little while, then she said 'Margaret is one in a thousand. How I wish I were like her! She would never have told you lies—been so deceitful——'

He stopped her protests with a kiss. 'Margaret is all right,' he said, 'but you are the girl I love—no matter what you did.'

She sighed happily. 'I will never deceive you about anything again—never!' she said.

'I am glad to hear you say that. And I feel I can trust you now. We have both had a lesson and must take it to heart. I promise not to be hasty with you again, and won't you promise to always tell me the truth about everything—no matter what it is?'

'I promise, Harold.'

Little did she think that her promise was to be put to the test at once.

'And now I have a bit of good news for you,' said Harold, 'what do you think? My mother has come in for a small fortune.'

He did not notice that the girl had turned suddenly pale, so eager was he to tell his news.

'She received a letter from Mr. Roper—you may have heard of him, he is a well-known solicitor in town—informing her that she was to receive ten thousand pounds from some person who wished to remain anonymous. No further details were to be given—she was just told it was from a well-wisher and a friend. Mr. Roper has asked her to call at his office after Christmas, and as tomorrow is Christmas Eve she will not have long to wait. But old Roper is a deep old boy, and she will get nothing out of him if his client has given him instructions to that effect. What do you think of it? Strange—isn't it?'

As she did not speak at once, he added, with a laugh: 'I told mother it must be from some old sweetheart, but she denied having had any except poor dad.'

Nora was making up her mind. She had just promised to tell him the truth. To have no secrets from him—he was to be told the truth about everything. She had not meant to tell him about her change of fortune until after they were married. But she knew now that he must be told at once. They must not commence this happy time with any secrets between them.

And so Harold heard with amazement all about her aunt's legacy. She told him that she had felt so glad to be able to repay the money to his mother.

'And you won't tell her—will you? Because if she knew she might not want to take the money and I do so want her to have it.'

'No—I won't tell her—for the present anyway. Maybe later when the two of you get to know and love one another—then we may tell her.'

Nora told him, too, about Grey Manor and of how she had disposed the rest of her fortune.

'But I must get Mr. Roper to make another Will now,' she said. 'I must leave my money to my husband!'

'Wait until we are married, darling, and then we can arrange everything. All you have to do now is to get well and strong as quickly as you can.'

A Christmas Gift for Nora

They were talking happily together, when Nurse Cullen entered the room. She had come upstairs unheard by Mrs. Gilfoyle, and her face when she saw Harold was ludicrous in its dismay and astonishment.

'What are you doing here?' she exclaimed. 'Who let you in? You must go at once!'

'It's all right, nurse,' replied Harold, with a smile. 'Miss Tiernan and myself are going to be married. Look at her! Isn't she better already?'

And Nurse Cullen, glancing at Nora, found herself gazing at such a different girl from the one she had left a few hours ago, that she knew he was right. Still he should not be there, and she was again telling them so when Teresa entered with a tea tray.

'Here's your tea, Nora, and Harold's name is in the pot!'

'Don't worry, nurse, it's all right. Come downstairs for your tea and we will explain everything.'

Bewildered, protesting still, Nurse Cullen allowed herself to be taken from the room.

'Pour out for me, Harold,' said Nora, happily, and then as she lifted the cover from a dish, she cried: 'Oh—muffins! How lovely—you are so fond of them!'

'And this time we will enjoy them together,' he said, 'not like the last time—do you remember?'

Did she not? And did she not remember another evening when she had had muffins toasted, waiting for him, and they were left to grow hard and cold, while a girl sat in darkness, alone?

But Harold was handing her one and helping himself while he hummed gaily: 'Tea for two—and two for tea!'

At Cross Roads Farm, Margaret was alone that night. Pat was spending the evening with Eileen. In fact he had gone to tell her the news which Margaret had imparted to him—the fact that she and Harold Hastings were not going to be married. Pat had been inclined to blame the man and threatened to let Harold know what he thought of him in no uncertain manner. But Margaret had put the matter so calmly before him, and had seemed so absolutely decided about it, that he really believed that the whole affair was her doing. She must have found out that she did not care for the fellow, and so had put an end to her engagement.

Both Pat and his future wife were very glad that Margaret was going to stay on at the farm. Eileen was fond of her, and she knew, too, that Margaret would be of great help to her.

'She is such a dear!' she said to Pat. 'I am very glad she is not going away.'

'Yes—she's a good sort—old Meg,' he replied in brotherly tones, 'I don't think I have ever seen her in a temper or put out in any way—always calm and placid.'

If he could have seen his sister at that moment he might have got a big surprise. Margaret was in her own room lying face downwards on the bed, hands clenched in agony, trying to fight her battle alone. She was seeing Harold and Nora together, as she knew they would be now, she could hear his voice talking to that other girl in tender tones, such as she had never heard from his lips; she could see them married, see their children growing up beside them; watch them going hand in hand through life together. And she saw her own lonely future—bleak, dreary, with nothing but duty and work before her

'Oh, God—help me to bear it! she cried. 'Help me—send me some bit of comfort some time.'

And her prayer was answered. The day was to come when she was to find her happiness in the sound of little voices calling: 'Auntie Meg! Auntie Meg! Where are you? We want you!'

And God sent her comfort in the clasp of a child's hand and the sound of children's voices.

www.ingramcontent.com/pod-product-compliance
Ingram Content Group UK Ltd.
Pitfield, Milton Keynes, MK11 3LW, UK
UKHW041411180426
11947UKWH00007B/67

9 781781 179291